All Things Right and Beautiful

Paul McCormack

Ichabod Dozer Press

ISBN 978-0-9854620-0-0

Tell Esther I'm sorry...

"[The idea of the Good is] the universal author of all things right and beautiful, parent of light and of the lord of light in this visible world, and the immediate source of reason and truth in the intellectual; and that this is the power upon which he who would act rationally, either in public or private life must have his eye fixed."

-Plato

"All things right and beautiful,
All creatures great and small,
All things wise and wonderful:
The Lord God made them all.

Each little flower that opens,
Each little bird that sings,
He made their glowing colors,
He made their tiny wings.

The rich man in his castle,
The poor man at his gate,
He made them, high or lowly,
And ordered their estate."

-Excerpted from the hymn *"All Things Right and Beautiful"*

Contents:

Prologue:

Dinnertime

I

This is the story of a man named Vernon, his two dogs he named Doc and Purvis (for unknown reasons), his young, attractive and completely vacant niece named Elise who came to live with him, and the ghost of a man who died in Vernon's house from a brutal bludgeoning in 1964. The ghost doesn't have a name, really. He's just dead but recurring, like a bad relationship.

A few other characters may drift in and out of this story, but ultimately it's about Vernon. Vernon was going through what pop psychologists would call a mid-life crisis, what philosophers might refer to as a time of existential awakening and examination, and what Vernon's ex-wife Rita called a goddamned fool-headed bunch of mish-mash. Rita really isn't in the story. She's recurring like the ghost, but she's not dead—she's just a bad relationship.

I should add the story also includes Vernon's neighbor. His name is Leonard, but he calls himself "Spook." But he's not the ghost, or dead, or even necessarily recurring. He's just in a punk band and he thought the name gave him some sort of credibility. Spook and Elise have sex a little later, but that's not important for now. Rita had left Vernon, and that is important because all Vernon had to his name as a result were his two dogs named affectionately (and mysteriously) Doc and Purvis.

Doc and Purvis were both neutered mutts. Rita once said she couldn't tell between Doc, Purvis and Vernon because all three came from poor breeding, stank when wet and had no balls. Vernon resented Rita for statements like that, which is why when she moved out Vernon intentionally dropped her box of collector plates marked "fragile."

Doc and Purvis knew about the ghost. They had seen him with his bloody and misshapen head lurching through the house, presumably looking for some sort of peace with eyes like eight balls and an agonizing limp from his shattered femur. The dogs liked the ghost. He smelled faintly of rancid meat. The dogs liked rancid meat.

Vernon didn't know about the ghost, but he did know about Elise who was in the process of moving into his guest bedroom for the summer. Vernon's sister, Kelly, and her husband decided Vernon needed comfort in his time of isolation and loneliness and they believed that the best cure for that would be to ship their eternally shiny and happy daughter to him under the pretense of some sort of cheerleading clinic. Vernon didn't much care aside from the fact Elise had already opened every blind and curtain in the house so every room was glaringly bright and everywhere she went had the faint odor of bubblegum and some sort of perfume. Doc and Purvis didn't much care either, except for the bubblegum smell. They couldn't smell the ghost when Elise was around.

"Uncle Vern, can I put up some posters so my room feels more like home? I know it's only for a few weeks, but I really feel like I'm far away from home right now." Elise asked things with too much explanation and always unconsciously showed off her legs, Vernon noticed.

"You are far away from home," he answered.

"Yeah, I know, but I need to feel like this is my home, not just a house. I need to be able to stay positive or I'm just going to fall apart at cheer camp," she said still showing off her legs.

Vernon didn't really know the difference between a house and a home. Of course he had been married. Married to Rita no less. All the things he had relished about being at home—walking around with no pants, smoking in his easy chair, falling asleep on the couch—had all disappeared within the first years of his marriage. Everywhere he went felt like a hotel now. He mostly kept his head down and didn't try to make any changes to anything, except when he dropped the box of plates. But that wasn't exactly to make a change.

"I don't care," Vernon shrugged.

"Oh thank you Uncle Vern!" Elise squealed as she threw her arms around her uncle, brushing her full chest and firm legs against him. Then she bounded up the stairs to her room.

Vernon shook his head. How people got ahead in life wasn't a mystery to him anymore. The Elises of the world got through by giving hard-ons to as many people as they could. The Ritas of the world got through by feigning pregnancy during their senior years of college and getting married to the Vernons. The Vernons got through just because they didn't know any better. The ghosts got through because they were Vernons who just didn't know better even after they were dead.

Vernon didn't realize he was a Vernon. The ghost knew Vernon was a Vernon. The ghost even knew the ghost was a Vernon. The ghost just didn't much care. The dogs liked having him around either way.

Vernon was in love. This was only the second time in his life he had been in love. The first time he had been in love was with Rita. He knew he had been in love because Rita had told him he was in love. It was right after she had told him she was pregnant and right before she told him to marry her. He had taken her word on the first and last things in that conversation, so it made sense to take her word for the love thing, too.

Vernon sat in his easy chair in front of the television, which was still turned off. He was thinking of Janice. Janice was the other woman Vernon had fallen in love with. She was a waitress at the cafe where Vernon had breakfast every morning. He knew he was in love with Janice because she always smiled widely when he came into the diner. She always called him names like "hon" or "sweetie" and even gave him free coffee when her manager wasn't around.

Vernon wasn't used to people being nice to him. Janice was always willing to chat with Vernon in the morning. She'd tell him all about what she had done the previous day and about her little dog, Pitsy. She had told him about her ex-husband and how she had moved away after she realized that he didn't love her for who she was anymore and how all she really wanted was a man who would listen to her and respect her.

Vernon would just smile and listen and nod. He admired her. He believed everything she said and thought that she was a wonderfully complex and fascinating character. He also admired her sturdy form. Janice was on the shorter side with bright eyes and wide curvy hips and a full bosom. She had dyed her hair dirty blonde. Vernon liked dyed hair. Rita had refused to dye her hair and when Vernon asked once, she told him to mind his own goddamned business. Vernon also liked how Janice smelled. It reminded him of a jewelry box his mother had kept on her dresser when he was a boy.

Vernon looked at his watch; Janice had just gotten off work. Vernon sighed. He had wanted to drop by at some other time than breakfast, just to say hi. That and he liked how she would chat with him and would always make sure his coffee was full and hot. Love was a sweet thing, Vernon decided.

Doc and Purvis sauntered through the living room, but Vernon didn't even notice. Doc and Purvis were looking for the ghost. They had just been shooed out of the kitchen by Elise who was fretting over some little thing. Doc had been first to pick up on the scent and Purvis was content to follow his comrade.

They found the ghost standing in the enclosed porch area, looking out. Their tails wagged happily as they flopped down on the wooden floor. The ghost just looked at them and gurgled through his crushed windpipe.

The ghost enjoyed looking out the window of the porch. Of course, he didn't see what Doc and Purvis saw. He didn't even see what Vernon or Elise saw. The ghost stood and watched as things were outside. The ghost didn't much care what was happening outside, he just liked seeing things that still existed and did existing things. Sometimes existing things just meant they hadn't stopped existing yet. That was part of the reason the ghost was wary of Vernon. He wasn't sure if Vernon existed or had stopped existing. The ghost suspected that Vernon did exist, at least in a minimal way, but he hadn't been sure until the day he had watched Vernon drop Rita's collector plates.

The ghost knew he didn't exist, except for a faint odor that kept the dogs as his constant companions. He didn't much care if he existed. He hadn't cared when he had existed and now that he didn't, he had found himself free to observe existing things. Of course the constant torment of his hideously beaten and battered frame left something to be desired, but, he reasoned, it was still better than a poke in the eye with a sharp stick.

Elise was trying to find her other cheerleading shoe. She had followed Doc and Purvis, suspecting they had smuggled it off and were in the process of chewing it to little bits. Upon imagining this Elise had felt herself thinking negative thoughts and had even stamped her foot in frustration. She had caught herself just in time. She took a deep breath and counted to twenty, just like she had learned in her favorite book, 40 Steps to a Happier You! by Margaux Maddux. Elise didn't go to church, but if there was a God, she believed She would happily stand behind everything Margaux Maddux said.

In Chapter 9, called "Finding Your Inner Strength", Margaux (Elise felt she knew her so well she wouldn't mind if she used her first name) had said, "The key to getting past negative thinking is realizing that you've got potential. It's your own inner value that makes you who you are and only by valuing yourself can you realize that potential. The only barrier you have to your dreams is your own negativity. When you find yourself doubting yourself and letting circumstances eclipse your inner beauty you've just got to stop, stand straight, take a deep breath and count to ten. Then blow out all that bad, used up air because that air is your negativity. Negativity is just a piece of your inner beauty that you need to let go of so you can take more in."

Elise thought that paragraph should be put on every school newspaper, annual, wall and locker in the world. She had even thought about getting a tattoo that said that, but then she realized it wouldn't fit on her ankle, so she got a butterfly instead. She had adapted Margaux's approach to negativity and had even added ten seconds to the time she should count. She had told her best friend back home, Missy, that if counting to ten was enough for normal people to get back in touch with their inner strength, then she would have to count to twenty, because she was naturally such a positive person that she'd have to work harder to get back.

Elise exhaled the air in a steady rush. She told herself it would be okay because if Doc and Purvis had gotten the shoe, then there would be little scraps and pieces of it around. She hadn't seen any, so it was probably just underneath something. She started looking for it again, starting in her room and working her way out. Sure enough, it had been hidden underneath a fluffy, pink overstuffed teddy bear she had just unpacked. She quickly got her uniform on and headed out. She was so happy and excited that cheer camp was about to begin. She loved the campus where they'd be working out and she loved her room and Uncle Vern was nice and there were so many things to be happy for. She gave the bear a big squeeze and then bounded down the hall and out the door.

She almost ran over Vernon on her way out the door. Vernon had been getting the mail and had been absent-mindedly looking over a flyer advertising carpet shampooing when he suddenly felt a pair of firm and soft arms wrap around his waist in a squeeze. Elise was grinning so widely her eyes were almost little slits. She pressed her ample chest into him and gave him a quick peck on the cheek. "This is going to be so much fun, Uncle Vern," she bubbled before she scampered on down the street.

Doc and Purvis looked up from their sprawled position on the floor with a look of minor irritation. Not only had their naps been interrupted, but now all they could smell was bubblegum and perfume. The ghost watched Elise indifferently. She jumped and hopped around so vigorously, but the ghost knew it was the lightest feathers that danced the most in the wind. No one was going to confuse her for anything more substantial than a feather anyway, the ghost figured.

When the ghost died in 1964 he had decided then and there to stay in the house. He hadn't thought his spirit would haunt those who had taken his life. He really didn't care too much that he was dead. If he had it to do over again, he probably wouldn't have chosen being beaten to death, but at this point it was inconsequential. The real reason he had stayed was because he wasn't fond of moving.

He had lived the better part of his life in that house except for a brief stint when he had moved to Cincinnati, Ohio. He hadn't cared much for Cincinnati and figured wherever he would be shuffled off to in the afterlife wouldn't be much of an improvement over his own house. He believed that if he would go to heaven it probably wouldn't be much better than Cincinnati. A lot of people made a fuss about going to Cincinnati before he had died in 1964, and it hadn't much impressed him, so why should heaven be any different?

The ghost dragged his dead leg and broken body down to the basement. He heard Doc and Purvis whining softly at the basement door when they realized they couldn't follow him. The basement is where two men had bashed in his brains back in 1964. It's also where Vernon kept his shotgun.

Vernon's shotgun sat on a dusty old workbench. It still had both barrels loaded and was covered with an old oily towel to keep it somewhat clean. Rita had hated the thing and forced Vernon to stash it away in the basement when they were married. Vernon really hadn't had a use for the shotgun until he was married, and then Rita had made him take it to the basement.

It was shortly after he and Rita had been married that he decided he was going to kill himself. He wasn't going to go out killing his wife and various other guests or family members like the folks he had seen on the news. Vernon had been quite rational about it, in fact. He had an extended "to do" list, mostly written by Rita, and the last thing on the list was, "Go to the basement and use shotgun." When he had written it down a few years ago Rita had just rolled her eyes and said, "You damn well better refinish those chairs my father gave us before you start doing your own little errands."

Refinishing the chairs was next to last on the list.

Lately, Vernon had been making progress on the list. Beside each completed task was a little red checkmark to indicate that it was done. Only three items didn't have a check by them: refinish the chairs, use the shotgun and build plate rack. Vernon had scratched out the plate rack item the day after he had dropped Rita's collector plates. He figured she wouldn't appreciate the effort anymore, anyway.

The ghost had seen the list and seen the items slowly shrink. First the gutters got cleaned, then the window in the attic was replaced, the garage and shed had been cleaned and neatly arranged and so on. The ghost wondered how long it would take Vernon to refinish the chairs. He didn't suspect it would take him long to use the shotgun as it took for the other items because the shotgun was really the only task that Vernon himself had felt strongly enough to put on the list.

The ghost wasn't too sure what to think about Vernon blowing his own head off in the basement. The ghost had thought about it quite a bit since he had seen the list. Knowing his luck, he reasoned, Vernon wouldn't have any ambition to go off to heaven or hell or wherever he was supposed to go when he died. That meant the ghost would have to share the house with Vernon. The ghost didn't mind sharing with Doc and Purvis—they were agreeable and didn't do anything but follow him around. Vernon, on the other hand, would probably want to sit down and have a chat. He'd probably want to sit and talk about that harpy of an ex-wife, or that waitress he'd been obsessing over lately, or something. Even if he didn't want to talk, the ghost didn't even like the idea of having to be seen by someone else. The ghost didn't like the idea of having to share the dogs either, but it was more the principle of the thing.

The ghost had been there almost thirty years before Vernon and if anyone had earned squatting rights, it was him. If Vernon was going to kill himself, he'd have to go home with Elise, the ghost decided. She was his family, and even if she wasn't aware that he was tagging along, it was her responsibility to find a place for him. The ghost felt himself getting frustrated. He started to think about Margaux Maddux and all her "inner beauty" bullshit. The ghost would have been just as happy if he hadn't heard Elise reciting that nonsense over the phone like some sort of mantra. "Negativity is just a piece of your inner beauty that you need to let go of so you can take more in." The ghost shook his head. Total bullshit, he thought.

II

Vernon was making a new friend. Once or twice a week he'd get a letter from his new friend and he'd have to scrawl his signature on something or call someone else to get some information. His new friend's name was Peter. Peter was an attorney. Peter was Rita's attorney. Rita didn't talk to Vernon anymore, but as soon as she stopped calling and writing, Peter began to talk to Vernon. Now everything Vernon had to say to Rita he was supposed to tell Peter instead. Vernon had called Peter yesterday to ask Rita if she knew where his good pants were. Peter said he didn't know and asked where was the last place he had seen them. Rita would have told him to leave her alone and close the door on his way out. Vernon already liked Peter more than Rita.

Vernon wondered if he was supposed to be in love with Peter now. After he had dropped her plates as she was stomping out the front door, Rita had yelled, "I'm the best thing that ever happened to you, you sorry piece of shit! You'll be sitting here all alone and then you'll realize how much you love me and then it will be too late!" Since Peter was supposed to be Rita now, Vernon wondered if he was supposed to realize how much he loved Peter. Vernon was getting a headache thinking about it, so he scrawled his name by a little 'x' on the form Peter had sent him and put it back in the envelope.

Doc and Purvis came and lay down by his feet. They had been scratching at the basement door for a few minutes and whimpering. They did that sometimes, but Vernon didn't much care. They seemed to like him enough and he could talk to them without having to call Peter. He scratched Purvis behind his ear absent-mindedly. Purvis just leaned into Vernon's hand and let his tail flop around happily. Doc yawned and then started licking off a plate Elise had forgotten by the chair.

Vernon looked at the clock. It was official; he was seven hours late for work. He was pretty sure he still had a job even though the office had stopped calling to see if he was coming last week. Vernon was an insurance claims adjustor. He got to tell people that their possessions were officially stolen, broken or defective and that they wouldn't be worth what they thought. He didn't go into the field much. His position mainly involved filing paperwork, sending out forms and talking to people on the phone that did what he did in little grey cubicles in Omaha.

The company had flown him out to Omaha once. Rita wanted to stay in a nice hotel, so Vernon paid the extra money to get a nicer place. A lot of people in the office talked about how nice Omaha was. Vernon hadn't cared much for Omaha, but Rita got to go shopping every day and sit in the hot tub every night. She even let Vernon sleep in the bed with her one night.

Before Rita left, she made Vernon go with her to see her therapist. Vernon didn't know why he had to go see Rita's therapist, but said he didn't mind if Rita went to see his proctologist. Rita told him to go to hell. Vernon just shrugged and followed Rita like Doc and Purvis followed the ghost.

The therapist was in her mid-thirties and had dusty brown hair. Her eyes hid behind a pair of large rounded eyeglasses. She had her hair tied up in a little bun like an old school marm. Vernon told her so. Rita just rolled her eyes and let out a sigh of disgust. The therapist just peeked over her eyeglasses disapprovingly.

The therapist took out a book from her desk and handed it to Vernon. It was called <u>40 Steps to a Happier You!</u> by Margaux Maddux. She said Vernon was unhappy and he was putting unnecessary strain on Rita. Rita and the therapist had discussed it at length and decided Vernon needed to have an intensive psychiatric evaluation, but until that time he should read the book to make Rita's life more bearable.

Vernon opened the book. It had chapter names like "Appreciate You!", "Beauty and Finding True Happiness", "Finding Your Inner Strength" and "Unleashing the Power of Your Positive Potential." Vernon asked if the book was an anthology of titles and headlines from women's magazines. Rita slapped Vernon in the arm. The therapist smiled with a syrupy disgust and told him to go home and read the book so his poor wife could have some peace of mind. She then told him to leave her office so Rita could talk more about him when he wasn't there.

Vernon didn't want to read the book. He was pretty sure he didn't like Margaux Maddux just from the picture and description printed in the back of the book. She had glossy lips, forged in an eternally over-enthusiastic smile and bright eyes. She reminded Vernon of the picture that Rita had included in her resumes where she was trying to look like a competitive, goal-oriented team player. At least that's what Rita had put as her personal description. Vernon thought that Margaux Maddux probably wouldn't dye her hair, either.

The caption below the picture said in part: "Margaux Maddux: author, singer, actress and public speaker has presented her message of health and beauty to millions of people in over 35 countries and her work has been translated into 15 languages.

"Ms. Maddux was a successful public relations representative for a major California theme park and resort. Her life took a dramatic turn when she learned she had a brain tumor. The doctors gave her only six months to live, but Margaux refused to give up. Margaux launched herself into a rigorous journey of spiritual awakening and self-discovery culminating in the release of her best-selling autobiography <u>A Better Me, A Better You.</u> Within six months of its publication, Margaux Maddux was recognized as the foremost authority in what she calls 'positivity and strength through inner healing and beauty'. What's more, the same day <u>A Better Me, A Better You</u> sold its 500,000th copy, Margaux was declared in full remission.

"Her second book, <u>40 Steps to a Happier You!</u>, is already being heralded as one of the most important books of the year. Already in its 12th edition, <u>40 Steps to a Happier You!</u> has already helped millions of people worldwide. Now that you have your copy, you could be next. Get ready for the life-changing effects of <u>40 Steps to a Happier You!</u>"

Vernon didn't want to just throw the book away. The therapist had charged him for it through Rita's bill. Last time the therapist gave Rita a book it had cost Vernon $80 for a skimpy 160 page paperback. He figured that since this book was over 250 pages, it would likely cost him over a hundred dollars. If she was going to charge him a hundred dollars for a paperback, it should at least be something he could read on the toilet, he figured. His niece was having a birthday soon, he recalled. Vernon decided she was going to get a hundred dollar book for her birthday this year.

This is where Spook comes into the story. While Vernon was debating whether he had his insurance job any more, Leonard, or Spook as he told everyone to call him, was in his garage rehearsing. He had his ancient and cracked electric guitar plugged into his big, staticy and Promethean amp. Spook liked to think of it as Promethean, at least. He envisioned himself as being the new disaffected prophet for an era that traded in its blood for bubblegum.

He was trying to get his band together again. They called themselves "Relative Faction" until they broke up a week before. Other than Spook "Relative Faction" featured Chad and Luis. Luis played bass and Chad was going to play drums when he had enough money to buy a drum set. For now they all set up in the garage and Chad just hit things together. They had broken up when Spook accused Luis and Chad for selling out after he saw them hitting on Vernon's niece, the cheerleader. It really didn't bother Spook that much, but he thought he had to maintain the image of "Relative Faction." Cheerleaders definitely weren't part of the "Relative Faction" mystique.

Since then, Spook had a change in vision and decided they should be a rock-a-billy punk band instead of the jazz-funk-fusion punk band that "Relative Faction" had been. He also had thought of a new name for the band. The band's new name was "The Chalupa Ponies" and their first album was going to be called "Never Mind the Sex Pistols, Here Come the Chalupa Ponies." After that he was going to do an album called "The Midnight Ride of the Chalupa Ponies." Then he was going to leave the band to do solo work.

Spook always had these things planned out in advance. His hopes for "Relative Faction" hadn't quite come true. He was hoping to impress an aspiring model/actress from school named Stacy and then show her how much cooler it was to be deep and brooding. Stacy had said Spook was cute after their show at a house party. Then Spook got drunk and Stacy's boyfriend beat the piss out of him.

"The Chalupa Ponies" were going to be different. Spook didn't care about Stacy anymore; he liked Elise. She always showed off a lot of leg when she talked to him and she took longer to say things then she needed to. Spook knew the signs and he knew that Elise was actually deeper then she let on. Deep, hot cheerleaders who dug him were definitely part of "The Chalupa Ponies" mystique, or at least he thought they should be.

He saw her reading this book all the time. He checked it out at the bookstore; it was in the "Self Awareness/Spirituality" section. She would be impressed with his brooding, artistic nature and then they would get together and then she might give him a hummer. Spook knew that acting deeper and more insightful than other people would pay off in the end.

Spook started firing off the chords to the new Chalupa Ponies single he was writing called "Political Maniacal." He craned his neck so he could look out the garage window into the neighbor's house. There was a window that ran along the hall of Vernon's house. Sometimes Spook was able to see Elise bounding back and forth while he was playing.

What Spook didn't see was the sour expression of the ghost who was looking out the window at him. Doc and Purvis were sitting behind him, watching him curiously. The ghost gurgled in disgust. Once when Vernon was out of town, Spook and his little band buddies had broken into the basement. They must have been stoned out of their minds because they sat down there for nearly three hours chanting some incoherent silliness trying to conjure up the ghost. The ghost had watched them for a while and then gone back up to look out on the porch, but their chanting was carried through the ancient heating ducts so it echoed through the house. It got to the point where the ghost wished he could be conjured just so he could give them a good licking. The ghost had never heard of such a thing: breaking into someone's house and chanting to try and call a ghost.

The ghost secretly wished Spook would elope with Elise so he could be left in peace with Doc and Purvis. Doc let out a yawn and stretched out. The back screen door opened and Vernon yelled for the dogs. They both took off for the backyard leaving the ghost to himself. With a final menacing gurgle, the ghost left the window and Spook to go to the basement.

In the basement the ghost saw the four unfinished chairs sitting on a plastic floor cover. There was a can of varnish and a package of sandpaper lying on one of the chairs. The ghost also noticed that the shotgun had been cleaned. The ghost just gurgled an irritated sigh and relived his murder again. One of the idiosyncrasies of being dead was he was forced to relive his beating whenever he didn't have anything better to do. Suddenly it was a cool evening in August 1964 and the ghost was suddenly looking at a hammer flying directly into his face.

Vernon was busily sanding away at the chairs in the basement when he heard a flurry of feet coming down the stairs. He looked up to see Elise, clad in her skimpy cheerleading outfit and three other nubile girls in similar dress. "Hi, Uncle Vern," she bubbled.

Vernon nodded in acknowledgement.

"Ohmigod, I had this great idea, Uncle Vern. Some of the other girls from out of town don't have any family or anything around and so I thought that they could just stay here. It would only be for a couple nights a week and we'll be quiet, I totally promise. I thought we could help around with cleaning and stuff to help pay for it. Please, Uncle Vern, it would mean so much to me."

Vernon was still trying to catch up with all the words that had just flown from Elise's mouth. By the time he realized the words "Um, okay," had slipped from his lips Elise and her friends had already made a shriek of excitement and raced up the basement stairs. Vernon sighed. He wished Janice were still at work. He wanted someone to chat at him and keep his coffee hot.

Elise and her friends Krissy, Karen and Shanice, bounded out the back door into the yard. As they spilled onto the back lawn, Elise noticed Leonard (she didn't know she was supposed to call him Spook yet) peeking at them through the window. She thought he was cute. Not in a handsome way but in an awkward and shy way. He always tried to act like he was cynical and bitter, but Elise thought deep down he just had too much negativity. If she could just make him read Margaux Maddux, he would start playing happy songs. That thought made Elise smile; she liked the thought of telling her friends back home about the cute boy who she got to write pretty songs.

She smiled at him and gave a little wave and a wink. She

saw his cheeks color red and then his head duck away from the window. She thought it was kind of sweet.

Spook saw her look at him. He saw the little look she gave. He knew beneath that syrupy sweet exterior there was a tigress waiting to be let out. Girls always dug the musician types; that's why he became a musician type in the first place. That and musician types weren't expected to do homework. He just needed an opportunity with her. He sat down and began working on a new song that would be just for Elise. He'd been thinking about it for a while, but now he knew that's what he needed to do. It was going to be called "Sweet Piece Elise".

III

The day began as innocently as any other day. The ghost stood on the porch with Doc and Purvis sleeping at his feet. He watched night things exist. Then he watched early morning things exist. The paperboy hurled the newspaper at the front step. Doc and Purvis woke up when the paper made its hollow thud on the front step. They both stretched and yawned and scratched. They sat with the ghost for a few more minutes and then got up and wandered around the house.

Purvis found the shoe first. It smelled like leather dipped in bubblegum and perfume. Purvis gave it a few tentative licks. Doc nudged in beside him and started gnawing on the shoelace. Purvis tried to push Doc off and began to chew on the toe. Doc growled and nipped at Purvis and Purvis decided to go back and sit with the ghost. Doc began to chew contentedly. Out of the corner of his eye he saw seven other shoes just waiting for him.

A couple hours later Vernon was awakened by a series of shrieks. He thought about seeing what it was about, but then he realized he really didn't care. Seconds later there was a frantic pounding on his bedroom door. Vernon exhaled deeply and rolled out of bed. He felt his hair sticking up straight on one side of his head. Rita would have made him comb it before she would have let anyone see him.

Vernon opened the door. In front of him were four girls standing in various forms of pajamas, faces ashen, eyes red and mascara running. Vernon wondered why they still had mascara on.

"Uncle Vernon, look," whimpered Elise as each of the girls held up a pair of shoes. Each pair had some sort of damage. On one, the toe had been chewed up. Another the tongue was ripped out. The sole was partially torn off another. Vernon stared at them through blurry, sandy eyes.

"They're ruined. They're all ruined," fumed another girl. Vernon didn't remember their names.

"What are we supposed to do, Uncle Vernon? We need these for cheerleader camp. We can't go with these. I know Doc and Purvis didn't mean to chew our things, but we don't have anything else we can use." Vernon realized that Elise even sobbed in a bubbly way.

"What are you going to do about this?" demanded another one of the girls.

Vernon just stood there, examining the shoes. "Um, I can buy you some new ones?"

"You just can't buy these anywhere, you know. I had to special order these!" fumed another girl.

"Um," was all Vernon could say.

"C'mon, we're all being so negative. We can try and find some new shoes. I'm sure we can get by just for today. Uncle Vernon said he'd pay for new ones. It will all be fine," said Elise putting on her brave face as she herded the girls back down the hallway. "We don't have to be there until after lunch today, anyway. Why don't you guys go out looking for some shoes now and I'll see if I can work something out with the ones here, okay?"

Vernon watched them walk down the hallway. He felt like he should feel bad, but he really didn't. If anything he thought it was kind of funny. Special shoes for cheerleading? He remembered a boy in school who had a clubfoot that needed special shoes. Maybe cheerleaders all had clubfeet, he thought. He thought about getting breakfast and seeing Janice, but decided that going back to sleep would be his best way of avoiding the angry club-footed girls down the hall.

Elise tried to keep a positive attitude in front of her friends. When they had gone she sat in the porch and cried for a few minutes. The ghost watched her for a few seconds. The ghost thought cheerleading shoes were silly, too. He thought crying over cheerleading shoes was very silly. He thought about reliving his murder again so he wouldn't have to listen to her sobs, but he decided to go back to the basement instead.

Elise kept repeating over and over in her mind what Margaux Maddux had said. "When circumstances in your life seem to make everything difficult, just remember: circumstances are just the fertilizer that beautiful flowers need to grow!"

Vernon had actually read that section before he had sent it to Elise for her birthday. He told Doc and Purvis about it. He told them that this crazy lady from someplace called California had said circumstances are the horseshit that fertilized flowers. Doc and Purvis hadn't been able to tell him what that was supposed to mean, either.

Elise thought she would find something else to do. She had to focus on something else before all this negativity ate her alive. She stepped outside and picked up the newspaper and looked at the headlines for a moment. She thought some news might be just what she needed.

Vernon awoke to another shriek. He figured it was just another extension of the shoe incident and rolled back over and went to sleep. He didn't want to hear about cheerleading shoes anymore.

Spook usually wasn't up this early, but Chad and Luis had just come by and the Chalupa Ponies had broken up. Chad and Luis decided to join another band with that little punk Corey Burton. Corey Burton was a faker and he couldn't write songs for shit, and in either case, he still did his homework. They were going to call themselves "Jimmy Hoffa's Missing Head." It was a typical sorry-ass junior high band name. Spook decided he would continue the Chalupa Ponies except it would just be him and whoever he felt like having around. That's how all the good bands worked anyway, he figured.

Spook looked out of his garage window and saw Elise sitting on the back step crying. He craned his neck, but didn't see her cheerleader friends around. Spook took a deep breath. This was his big chance; the time to strike was now.

Elise looked up with her blurry puffy eyes and saw Leonard standing in front of her. She tried wiping her eyes and smiling. She didn't want to look like she was dwelling on the negative.

"Wassup," said Spook.

Elise sniffled and shook her head. "It's nothing."

"Well, if you, you know, want to talk or something, I'll be over in the garage. My name is Spook. Don't worry about coming in if you hear some music going or something, I'm just working on some new songs," Spook said with his best indifferent air.

"Thank you," Elise sniffed.

Spook was about to turn to leave when Elise suddenly stood up and embraced him. Spook embraced her back with a relieved smirk. No one could resist the Spook, he thought.

"I'm sorry. You're just so sweet. I just don't know what to do. She's dead," whispered Elise.

"Who's dead?" asked Spook.

Elise just shook her head and began crying again. She handed him the newspaper and pointed at a page before continuing her sobs.

Spook read the headline: "Self-help Guru Dies at Convention".

"Margaux Maddux, acclaimed writer of <u>A Better Me, A Better You</u> died yesterday. She had been giving a presentation based on her latest best seller <u>40 Steps to a Happier You!</u> in Pasadena when she collapsed. One eyewitness reported, 'She was just telling us how to achieve our true beauty potential and she just stopped and got this funny look on her face. She asked if someone was burning cabbage and then she just fell over.'

"Initial results indicate that a brain tumor was the likely cause of death. Dr. Santiago Belize, head of neurosurgery at Holy Virgin Medical Center indicated the symptoms of Ms. Maddux's tumor would have likely gone unnoticed aside from possible episodes of euphoria and delusions."

"She knew everything. She was like a mother to me and I never even got to go see her. I had reservations to go see her with my mom in Tampa," sobbed Elise.

Spook put his arm around her. She felt so warm and firm. He knew that she wanted him. "It's okay. Here, let's go over to my garage. I've been working on a song for you. It'll cheer you up."

Elise felt so happy she had been right about Leonard. He was a warm and caring individual who seemed to really be at peace with his own inner beauty. She liked how it felt when he had his arms around her.

The ghost couldn't stand anymore. He chose to relive his murder instead of watch where the encounter was undoubtedly heading. He saw the hammer and felt the initial stunning blow in his temple. Couldn't be any worse than watching those two, the ghost thought as his assailants crushed the life out of him for the thousandth time.

Spook led her back to the garage and played "Sweet Piece Elise" for her and then they talked for a little while. That is when they had sex. The details aren't really important, but they did have sex.

As Elise lay on the garage floor with Spook she played with his arm hair and thought about how positive she was feeling. She would get the girls together and they would skip cheer camp today and do something really special for Uncle Vernon. Then she would go to her room and write her best friend at home, Missy, and tell her all about Leonard and how sweet he was and how they had slept together.

Spook was lying face down. He felt Elise messing with his arm, but he didn't much care; he was falling asleep. He would show those little fucks in "Jimmy Hoffa's Missing Head" when he showed up with Elise at his next gig. They'd all wonder how he had snagged her and then he'd tell them how they had done it in his garage because she was so turned on by "Sweet Piece Elise". That would show them. If not, maybe he'd start studying accounting instead, it all seemed about the same to him either way. There would just be more homework in accounting.

Vernon finally rolled out of bed about two in the afternoon. He hadn't heard any shrieks in a while so he thought it was probably safe to come out. He walked stiff-legged down the hall. Doc and Purvis were sitting in the porch area again. Their tails wagged vaguely when they saw him. Vernon poured a glass of milk and sat down at the kitchen table.

He sat there for a minute, wondering if he should call Peter, just to let him know he was thinking of him. He wasn't really thinking of Peter, but Rita had made him do that every hour on the hour when he was at work before he had broken her plates and she had left. He really hadn't been thinking of her, but he got in the habit of calling her. She never seemed to be happy to hear from him, but if he didn't call she'd throw things at him when he got home. Vernon was thinking about calling Peter when he thought he heard something coming from the basement.

He listened for a moment, and he definitely heard something in the basement. Elise and her friends were supposed to be at cheer camp. Vernon wondered if the same people who had broken into the basement when he and Rita had gone to Omaha were back. Vernon put on a pot of coffee. If they had broken back into the basement, the least he could do was offer them a pot of coffee.

When the coffee was ready he grabbed the pot and three cups. He could only really carry three cups at once and almost dropped one anyway. He thought about letting it fall, but decided it wouldn't be as rewarding as dropping collector plates. He descended the stairs and peeked around the corner. What he saw turned his face white. He ended up dropping the coffee cup anyway.

IV

Standing in front of Vernon were four girls, each wearing cutoff shorts and old t-shirts. They all had their hair tied back or were wearing hats. It took him a moment to realize that one of them was Elise. She beamed at him, a streak of varnish running across her cheek.

"Surprise, Uncle Vern," she bubbled.

Standing in the middle of the room, plain as day, were four freshly refinished wooden chairs. Vernon scanned the room desperately trying to find the ones that Rita's father had given them, but he couldn't see them. There were only the four varnished chairs standing exactly where the old unfinished ones had stood.

The ghost shook his disfigured head. Good luck trying to get him to go with Elise now, the ghost thought. The poor fellow had gone off his nut. The ghost hadn't had any company since 1960, not counting his visitors in1964, and he wasn't really looking forward to getting Vernon now. Why couldn't he get Doc and Purvis? They were as much company as he cared to have.

Vernon felt something rising in his stomach and working its way up his spine. He vaguely remembered the sensation. It was hot and sweaty and burning. It wasn't a newfound appreciation for life. It wasn't even the desire to live. It was irritation: pure, hot and churning irritation.

It had been so long since he remembered feeling anything other than tired and vaguely itchy that he didn't know exactly how to react. Elise and her little cheerleader friends didn't seem to notice and instead continued with the finishing touches on the chairs. After a moment, Vernon nodded stiffly and walked back up the stairs.

When Elise and her friends came flying back up the stairs twenty minutes later they found Vernon sitting at the table staring at a "to-do" list, shaking his head and muttering "Goddamn plate rack" over and over. Elise had no idea what he was talking about, but she knew it couldn't be about her. She and her friends gathered their things and went to Shanice's dorm room to have pizza and watch a video of the three previous years' cheerleading finals.

The ghost had decided to relive his murder another two or three times after he saw the chairs. Now he was looking around the house to see if he could find Vernon's body, with or without a head, lying around. When he came to the kitchen he saw Vernon staring at his to-do list. Doc and Purvis cocked their heads and watched Vernon whispering the same line over and over. They wanted dinner, but it didn't look like Vernon would be feeding them for a while. The ghost sighed and saw the hammer strike him and a crimson streak of liquid go flying off his head into the darkness of the basement.

Vernon tried to call Peter, but Peter was gone for the day. Janice was gone, too. If seeing the finished chairs had filled him with dread or relief or anything other than irritation he would have been happy. He would have known exactly where he stood in relation to the infinite somewhere he had signed himself up for on the last line of Rita's "to-do" list. But he was just irritated. It was his project. They were his chairs to finish and when he had finished them, then he would finish the list. But Elise had finished the chairs. For a moment he thought about trying to talk her into finishing the list for him, too. Upon picturing it he could only visualize Elise giggling at him as if he had told a joke and then telling him something Margaux Maddux had said. Hearing Margaux Maddux would probably be enough motivation for him to finish the list himself, but for now he didn't know what he wanted to do.

The four of them waited in the kitchen, expectantly, for three hours. Well, Vernon, Doc, and Purvis waited expectantly. The ghost would wait for a little while and then die again and then would wait for little longer and then repeat the process.

Finally as dusk began settling over the neighborhood and the kitchen turned an eerie bluish-grey, Vernon stood up. He made a quick note on his list and headed down to the basement. Doc and Purvis followed him and the ghost pulled his shattered leg, and broken pelvis along behind them. When the ghost arrived he saw Vernon standing by the workbench where the shotgun lay underneath its oily rag. This time the ghost didn't die again, but watched with a mix of anticipation and dread. Doc and Purvis wagged their tails limply hoping that their presence would remind Vernon to fill their food dishes.

Vernon was scribbling on a piece of paper at the workbench. He thought he faintly smelled rancid meat, but didn't think much of it. He did smell rancid meat. The ghost was standing right over his shoulder, looking to see what Vernon's final words to the world were going to be. What he saw was a series of numbers and a couple of lines.

Vernon pushed the shotgun aside and grabbed a piece of wood and a tape measure and placed them squarely on the table. At the top of the piece of paper he had scrawled "Plate Rack." The "to-do" list was his and he had to finish it. It was his list. No one else would be able to do it because of the last item. And he'd be damned if some perky cheerleaders would ruin it for him. The list just wouldn't mean anything if it wasn't all his. He'd finish the plate rack and then give it to Peter as a surprise. Then he'd finish the list. But for now, he had to finish the plate rack. It had been on the list and he never should have crossed it out. It was all about the list.

Doc and Purvis sprawled out on the basement floor and wondered if they'd ever get their dinner.

Time and Tide

I

This is more about Vernon. You might remember Vernon; he had two dogs. They were good dogs. Their names are still (inexplicably, I might add) Doc and Purvis.

Vernon hadn't seen Doc or Purvis for quite some time. He wanted to see them. He definitely wanted to see Janice, his waitress. He didn't want to see Rita. Rita was his ex-wife. Vernon was sitting in a small white room with Rita. Vernon began to believe in Hell.

"Now Vernon, you've put me through hell."

Apparently Rita was thinking along the same lines, Vernon thought. Maybe there was a reason they had been married after all, he pondered. "Dr. Nash says you've been taking your meds again and that if you keep up your good behavior you can go home soon."

Rita began sobbing. "Why do you keep doing these things to me, Vernon? Let me go. I'm happy. Me and Peter are getting married and there's nothing you can do about it."

Vernon vaguely remembered Rita telling him that she was marrying the lawyer that Vernon was supposed to be in love with. He had considered being jealous, but instead just signed by a little red ink x and sent it off. He figured that would suffice for a wedding gift for the two of them. Vernon lowered his head and tried to make the buzzing in his head stop. Rita was still carrying on.

"I know the divorce was hard on you Vernon, but I need space to breathe. I need to be free and Peter makes me free. If you could find some of your happiness instead of trying to take away all the happiness around you, maybe you would be happier."

Vernon thought the entire statement was pretty redundant. Doc and Purvis would have, too. He wanted to take them for a walk, but patients were only allowed to go outside on the enclosed catwalk for smoke breaks twice a day. Vernon didn't smoke.

Everything had fallen apart almost two months before. Vernon's niece, Elise, had run across a list on the kitchen table during her final week staying with him. By the list was an immaculately finished and polished little plate rack.

The week before Elise found the list, an angry man went to a busy department store in a busy mall and angrily shot his busy boss who had busily fired him the previous day. Elise had stayed up all night rereading Margaux Maddux (who was now quite dead) trying to find out why someone would do such a horrible thing. After many hours of positive reflection, Elise, with the help of the late Margaux Maddux, had determined that the kind of person who did such a thing had so much negativity inside that they lost their soul.

When she mentioned her theory to Vernon, Vernon had only replied that she had apparently never had a job before and that souls were easier than pocket change to lose. Elise was instantly suspicious that her beloved Uncle Vernon was under the influence of negativity.

Needless to say, when she found the list with every item checked off except "Go to the basement and use the shotgun," Elise naturally assumed that Vernon had completely flipped and was going to, under the cover of night, lure Elise and her friends Krissy, Karen and Shanice to the basement and do away with all of them after acting out some sort of sick ritualistic sex fantasy.

During the committal hearing the judge had asked Vernon if he had ever considered harming himself or others. Vernon had shrugged and replied that stranger things had happened. It was true, after all. Vernon was trying to humor everyone, but quite frankly the thought of being stuck in the basement with the four cheerleaders did make some sort of impulsive mass killing seem slightly less arduous.

At the hospital it took staff four days to realize Vernon wasn't heavily medicated. For the most part Vernon would just sit and watch the television in the main room or play checkers by himself next to the window. Whenever the staff asked him if he needed anything he would just ask if someone could bring his dogs by. The head nurse, a large black woman who would have been intimidating had it not been for her wide smile and quick wit, would just grin sympathetically and pat Vernon's hand and tell him he wasn't at home anymore, but that as soon as he got out he could see his dogs again.

After the fourth day, the doctors and nurses finally realized their error and quickly began feeding Vernon a steady diet of little white pills and strangely colored gelatin tablets. Vernon became used to the steady influx of medications and soon began to believe that there was no meal that didn't begin and end with an "-ine" "-ax" "-ium" "-zone" or "-done" of some sort.

Over the next few weeks Vernon realized that sleeping a lot was a good thing. Sometimes it was the only thing. He didn't wonder if he was supposed to be at work anymore, or if Janice missed filling his coffee. He would lie in bed and groggily marvel at the wide variety of colors around him that were all considered "off-white."

The only place Vernon was allowed to go that wasn't off-white was Dr. Nash's office. Dr. Nash had Vernon come in to see him a couple times a week to talk about how he was feeling. Vernon would tell him that he wanted to see his dogs again and Dr. Nash would nod approvingly. "I'm glad to see you're concerned about things outside yourself, Vernon," he would say. "When I talked to your ex-wife Rita she seemed very concerned that you didn't care about anything at all except trying to get her back."

Vernon would nod thoughtfully. He didn't want Rita back. He didn't want Rita to visit him at the hospital anymore either. When he told Dr. Nash, Dr. Nash shook his head disapprovingly. "She's very concerned for you Vernon. She's afraid that you might hurt yourself or someone else. I think that talking with people who are concerned about your well-being helps you understand the world you live in better, don't you?"

Vernon always nodded when Dr. Nash ended a sentence with "Don't you?" Rita used to do that, except she would end her sentences with "Is that what you want?" and Vernon would have to shake his head no or have something thrown at his head. If Rita and Peter didn't work out, maybe Dr. Nash would marry Rita, Vernon mused.

After their session, Vernon would agree to let Rita stay on his visitor's list and every week like clockwork Rita would come in to visit him. Rita would always start by smiling and asking how he was. It reminded Vernon of the time she was trying to convince him to take her to Omaha. Before long, though, she would be crying and talking about herself and how, even behind locked doors isolated from Doc and Purvis, Vernon was ruining her life.

"At the rate you're going, someday you're going to go completely off your rocker and start shooting people. And then everyone I know is going to watch the news and say to me: Rita, isn't that your ex-husband? Why did he shoot all those people Rita? What kind of person are you to allow your ex-husband to up and start shooting people like that, Rita?

"Can you imagine what they would say about me? Is that what you want?"

Vernon had to catch himself; he almost nodded like he was with Dr. Nash.

II

One of the little red x's Vernon had signed by had been to appoint Peter power of attorney. Since Vernon was quite clearly mad, Rita convinced Peter to take steps to make sure Vernon could pay his own medical bills instead of relying on Rita's goodwill and understanding. Rita had Peter sell the house and set up a trust fund so that Vernon would be able to pay his bills, but not buy a bunch of guns to kill people with.

Rita and Peter sold the house off. Peter kept 15% as a broker fee and used the remainder to set up the fund with interest payments going to Rita as a management fee. Peter and Rita then went to Cincinnati for a couple of weeks.

Doc and Purvis didn't go to Cincinnati. They went home with Elise. They didn't want to go with Elise. She still smelled like bubblegum and perfume and the dogs still didn't like bubblegum or perfume. They liked rancid meat, which is what the ghost smelled like. The ghost, however, was still at the house that no longer belonged to Vernon. And Doc and Purvis, like Vernon, were now under the care, custody and control of forces they could not comprehend.

After years of relative quiet, Doc and Purvis were suddenly subjected to the constant and manic attention of Elise's younger siblings Carson and Renee. Carson and Renee were four and five, respectively and found no greater pleasure in life than treating their newly-acquired pets like hyperactive puppies. Whenever Doc and Purvis managed to sneak away long enough to steal a quick nap they would be awakened by thundering footsteps and clamor of the children. Or, worse yet, the clamor wouldn't wake them and they'd awaken to Carson and Renee physically throwing themselves onto their unwitting playmates.

Elise for her part wasn't much better. She insisted on taking both dogs out on her insanely long jogging trips across the countryside. In their younger days both Doc and Purvis would have appreciated the activity lavished upon them, but now they would have rather smell the ghost and chew on something. Instead they found themselves being forced to run alongside the cheery bubblegum and perfume creature that had taken them away from the ghost. Doc and Purvis didn't know about hell, but they weren't happy with their new living arrangements.

The ghost knew about Hell. He was convinced that he had somehow slipped through a crack and ended up there. Gone were his constant companions, Doc and Purvis. Even the ineffectual lump that was Vernon was gone. Now the ghost was living in an earth-tone nightmare complete with designer furniture, two purebred Persian cats and a young married couple who drove an SUV and still had sex all over everything.

The trouble had begun early on. The ghost had decided to watch things exist on the front porch for a while one morning. To his horror, when he had managed to drag his mangled leg up the stairs, through the living room and to the porch he wasn't greeted by the burning haze of the sunrise, but by the animalistic grunts of the new homeowners. Disgusted, the ghost relived his death three times in a row, each time looking forward to the slight glint off the hammer head as his blood made it shimmer in the dim light of the swinging overhead utility light in the basement that night in 1964.

When the new couple wasn't rearranging, remodeling or somehow defacing the ghost's home, they were inviting that little punk Spook over. When the wife was away, the husband would have Spook over and together they would get stoned and mess around on an acoustic guitar. The husband liked Spook because he reminded him of how he used to be. The man was still like Spook, except he was balding, married and desperately trying to convince himself that he was indeed a free-thinking man.

Spook, for his part, was like the man, except he still had his hair and wasn't married. Spook just liked the free weed and thought the guy's wife was kinda hot. When the Chalupa Ponies made it big he would probably nail her and then just leave. That's what a rock star did, after all. That and Spook was trying to prove to himself that he was edgy and angsty.

Spook had actually been angsty, although it was not because he was grappling with a sense of nausea stemming from his own realization of existence, or from the burden of free will. It was because Elise had moved back and hadn't even called him once. Spook had spent long torturous nights trying to find the exact power chords that expressed his sense of loss, heartbreak and disillusionment to no avail.

He had proudly proclaimed to all who would listen that he and Elise had made hot, nasty, sweet, sweet love together. No one believed him, but they all mostly pretended to be interested. A few actually were interested in the sordid details, but then again, there's always a market for sordid details. It didn't help Spook's claim that Elise never showed up to any of his gigs. She had even been seen at a show that "Jimmy Hoffa's Missing Head" had played, which had driven Spook insane with jealousy and angst-like tantrums for a week.

Elise would just smile and say she hadn't realized that Spook was playing—after all, he didn't have actual "gigs" he just played at open-mic night at the local coffee house. The other times Elise said she was busy with cheer camp duties, and of course, in the end, making statements to the police, social workers, Rita and Rita's fiancé Peter.

Spook watched the night unfurl from his garage window. He had been working out a tune which was either called "Periwinkle Death" or "Elise is a Dumb Bitch Who Doesn't Care About Anyone But Herself" but was having a problem with the bridge, mainly because he wasn't sure which lyrics he was going to use.

He noticed Elise and her little cheerleader friends had gathered, speaking in whispers on the back door steps. They all had grave expressions and were nodding solemnly as Elise was gesturing in tight, frantic little circles. The other girls halfway tried to hide behind some bushes by the alleyway as Elise talked in hushed tones into the cordless phone she had taken with her.

She hung up the phone and nodded to her friends. She then did her best sneaky entrance back into the house. What happened next was only fully witnessed by the ghost, who, even if he could have been compelled to tell his story would have only blown some congealed blood bubbles through his collapsed trachea.

Elise came flying out of the house, Doc and Purvis reluctantly in tow squealing "Run Doc! Run Purvis! Run to safety!"

Her friends gave little screams of fright and frantically gestured for Elise to join them in their shrubbery of safety. As soon as Elise released their collars, Doc and Purvis ambled back to the steps and flopped down irritably waiting to be let back in. Elise was about to go back after them, but her friends grabbed her and pulled her back.

Vernon appeared at the back door, suspecting the screams of the poorly concealed cheerleaders were yet another plaintive wail about their unclad clubfeet. The twilight was casting a charcoal haze over the scenery and Vernon was squinting to see what the fuss was about. Doc and Purvis yawned and angled towards Vernon's feet aiming for the back door. Suddenly a spotlight cut through the dusk and shone right in Vernon's eyes.

"Run Doc! Run Purvis! He's crazy!" came a wail from the invisible world beyond the light.

"Just shoot him! He's insane!" came another squeal.

Vernon was puzzled, but stepped aside to let the dogs in anyway.

"Please doggies, don't go in!" came a scream.

At this point Spook saw either Krissy, Karen or Shanice faint—he couldn't remember which one was which. The light was from the spotlight of the first responding police unit. Vernon waved nonchalantly at the light and closed the door. Elise made a mad dash for the door but was tackled by the police officer. As Vernon closed the door, he heard Elise's anguished scream of "Noooooooo!"

Vernon thought it was odd, but decided to make a can of soup and a cheese sandwich.

When had Elise called 911, she didn't calmly explain the situation or her concerns to the dispatcher. The extent of her message was her full name, her address and "He's crazy. He's got a gun and he's going to kill us!"

Needless to say, the dispatcher was a bit alarmed. What Elise hadn't realized was that, while leaving the phone off the hook would keep Vernon from making any calls, it also kept the dispatcher from being able to verify the actual situation and well-being of the involved parties. As a result, a small army of the local police, including a S.W.A.T. team, bomb squad and a throng of counselors, clergy and medical staff converged on the small house all prepared for a worst-case scenario to play out in the quiet neighborhood.

By the time Vernon, Doc and Purvis on his heels, emerged from the house coughing and trying to wave the clouds of tear gas away with a cheese sandwich and balancing a bowl of soup in his other hand, Vernon was greeted with an arsenal of pepper spray, tazers, handguns with a wide selection of caliber, various rifles, shotguns, batons and a dazzling array of ill-will. Vernon had dismissed all the noise outside as the doings of his niece and the kid next door who did everything too loudly. As his face was being pushed into the lawn and his arms and legs were being adjusted into various uncomfortable positions, Vernon began to wish that he had finished his plate rack a couple days sooner.

The irony, of course was that Vernon hadn't finished the plate rack at all. The plate rack that Elise had seen by the list was one that Vernon had finally broken down and purchased. His own was in various developmental stages in the basement—none of them able to live up to the standards he had envisioned for a plate rack. For most of the police action Vernon had been waiting for his soup to heat in the basement where he was redesigning the plate rack using some of the ideas he had stolen from the mass-produced one on the kitchen table.

Dr. Nash wanted Vernon to talk about the plate rack. Dr. Nash was convinced that plates and their associated racks were some sort of metaphor for either Vernon's mother or his penis—he was still trying to determine which. Vernon would shrug and start to once again lay out the evolution of the plate rack. The first one was too bulky and only held three plates. The second one was smaller, but plates fell out of it too easily and so on. Dr. Nash would sit, furiously scribbling notes to himself with each passing description. Vernon wondered if Dr. Nash had also had problems with plate racks.

Dr. Nash would eventually let out a triumphant little chuckle and stop writing. Vernon would wait for Dr. Nash to finish gloating over his latest psychoanalytical triumph and then would ask if he could go home yet.

Dr. Nash would smile sympathetically and answer "I think you've made wonderful progress, but there's still a lot that you need to work through. I'd like to see how you're progressing, so I think you should stay here for another week and see what happens. Don't you?"

III

The ghost was tired. He had lived a fair number of years, and been dead a fair number as well and, if prompted he could name a number of topics that could potentially count as interesting, fascinating and perhaps even captivating. None of those topics included or involved Wayne and

Yvonne. Wayne and Yvonne lived in his house now. The ghost didn't much care if they were interesting. Vernon wasn't interesting and that had in no way distressed the ghost. On the contrary, when things appeared to actually happen with Vernon the ghost grew nervous.

But then Vernon didn't think he was interesting either.

Wayne and Yvonne had a different worldview and instead of being interested in normal things like car payments, cleaning the gutters or trying to get the lock on the bathroom door to work properly, they were preeminently interested in Wayne and Yvonne. The ghost had spent miserable weeks listening to Wayne and Yvonne discuss how progressive and how much smarter they were than anyone else. They, after all, were the new generation—the technically savvy and cynically cool leaders of the great *status quo*-ing. Their education made them more literate to "real world" applications with enough of the "classical" buggery that made them well-rounded sophisticated individuals.

What the ghost quickly learned is that meant that they wanted to make money, and discuss things that hadn't mattered, or were really even matters of debate, for a century. They also had no desire to purchase anything unless they were supposed to not want to purchase it. They had a penchant for anything sold with contempt. And, had either of them broken a sweat doing actual work instead of their scheduled weekly yoga sessions, gym workouts or obscenely organized sexual encounters, they would have likely keeled over from the excruciating sense of actual accomplishment.

The ghost hated Wayne and Yvonne. The ghost hadn't hated anything that passionately since the New York Yankees rallied from a 3-1 game deficit to beat the Milwaukee Braves in the World Series in 1958. Normally the ghost wouldn't have cared, but he'd put money on the game. And they'd waited until the eighth inning to put it away, no less. The Yankees liked talking about themselves a lot, too. But the Yankees never threatened to have a baby.

It had started innocently enough—or as innocently as pure evil could be, the ghost reflected. She had returned home from her job with a small teddy bear with a pink ribbon around its neck. Normally, that would have disgusted the ghost enough into voluntarily feeling the steel-toe boot kick his teeth in as he lay stunned in his basement, blood flowing from the hammer wounds in his head. Unfortunately, each reliving seemed to take less and less time and instead of the comforting and familiar death at the hands of strangers, he found himself in the world of Wayne and Yvonne—materialistic tyrannical überpigs of his little universe.

The ghost had intentionally not learned their names for as long he could. He hadn't learned Vernon's name for two years after he had moved in, but Wayne and Yvonne could barely go three minutes without proclaiming themselves to each other.

"Oh Wayne, have you seen the keys?"

"Yvonne, I can't believe that woman at the antique shop actually talked to you. Did she finally decide to give you a price for the gravy boat?"

"Hi, we're Wayne and Yvonne. We're not at home right now but if you leave your name and number, we'll be sure to get back to you," Yvonne's voice would giggle from the unholy little electronic box.

It was bad enough to hear them when they were there, but that infernal machine kept resurrecting their obnoxious self-involved voices every twenty minutes as one of their loyal self-involved followers would call. Even worse was when they would leave little cute messages for each other using their pet names: ragamuffin and love urchin.

And then there were the cats. They were arrogant fluffy white bundles of filth. Where Doc and Purvis would follow dutifully and offer their company, Kurt and Courtney would just lick themselves or occasionally hiss in the ghost's direction. One of the little beasts even had the gall to face the ghost as he was limping through and defecated directly in his path and then pranced off in a self-righteous trot. They would all have to be destroyed.

Of course the ghost wasn't able to do anything to anything. After a particularly brutal night of multiple sessions of romantic entanglement between Wayne and Yvonne in (but not limited to) the kitchen, the porch, the basement, the stairs, all three bedrooms and the entryway, the ghost finally resolved to take action.

Taking action was not the ghost's strong point. The ghost, after all, was like Vernon except dead. Vernon at that very moment was in awe at the great rainbow of color in his room that ranged from ivory, to bone to a miraculous cream derivative. Vernon didn't know what to do with himself aside from look at all the whiteness around him. It was either that or look out the window for Rita to come and tell him what he had done wrong. Perhaps it was time to do something, he mused absent-mindedly before he settled back into a drug-induced haze of near-sleep.

Spook was no longer called Spook. His nametag said "Leonard" in tight little black letters. Leonard decided that all rock stars had to grudgingly assist the system so they could become angsty and have enough money to buy new amps. So Spook became Leonard and started getting up every morning to call people on the phone and try to sell them things they didn't want while they were trying to eat, or sleep or do something that wanted to do much more than talk to him. He'd shuffle into his cubicle with his cup of coffee and set his phone up. After that everyone he talked to became "sir" or "ma'am" and he was always graciously asking for a moment of their time and then rambling on, whether they had opted to give him a moment of their time or not.

For the top producer there was an all-expense paid to Cincinnati for the winner and a friend. There was a cute girl who sat in the cubicle next to him. Leonard wanted to win the trip and then take her along. Chicks dug that kind of thing. That would add to his indie cred—obtaining easily what others worked so hard for, not to mention that it would pay for his new amp. That and she would probably put out. Girls putting out was definitely part of the Chalupa Ponies mystique Leonard figured as he swatted at the alarm clock by his bed.

The sun wasn't even up yet and Leonard was forced to reconcile his easy-going cool rocker guy "Spook" persona with his slave name at work by seven AM "Leonard" persona. So far he wasn't too fond of his "Leonard" persona—it had to get up too early; it was supposed to be interested in meeting sales goals, being a good employee to a company that was likely pure evil and, most unnerving of all, it was not very likely to score with the ladies. Leonard swore to himself silently and pried himself out of the bed and hobbled to the shower as the sky began to turn color.

As the sun rose the ghost stepped foot outside his house for the first time since 1964. Gurgling irritably and unsure of exactly how to proceed, he limped and lurched down the dimly lit street. Kurt and Courtney sat at the window watching him while licking themselves.

Meanwhile, Vernon was dreaming of a flying wallaby named "Herbie" in his stiff and flat hospital bed. Doc and Purvis were being tethered for another crack of dawn jogging session with Elise. Dr. Nash was pouring over his notes from his previous sessions with Vernon in his home study.

And somewhere Yvonne and Wayne had sex.

IV

Dr. Nash was unhappy. Vernon had been under his care for nearly ninety days and he was still unable to tell whether the plate rack was supposed to be Vernon's mother or his wee-wee. Vernon for his part wasn't making things easier; whenever Dr. Nash would start a line of questioning to determine whether the plate rack was supposed to be his mother or his nether organ, Vernon would agree complacently with whatever was asked and Dr. Nash found himself under a mountain of contradictory evidence.

Vernon didn't think much about plate racks anymore, except when he was with Dr. Nash.

Vernon saw Dr. Nash becoming more and more frustrated with each of his visits to the faux-wood paneled office. Vernon thought Dr. Nash would probably be happier making a birdhouse or an ashtray or something.

"Okay Vernon, we're going to try something a little different today," Dr. Nash said calmly.

Vernon shrugged and vaguely wondered if he had gotten his after-breakfast, pre-lunch medications yet.

"Alright Vernon, I'm going to say a word, and I want you to say the first thing that comes to your mind. Do you understand?"

Vernon nodded, and so Dr. Nash's new game commenced with Dr. Nash saying a word in a cautious monotone with Vernon answering in his tired monotone.

"Wife." "Rita."

"That's good Vernon, just keep answering them like that. How about: Dog?"

"Doc and Purvis."

"Black." "Dark."

"Mother." "Pie."

"Interesting. Okay, one more Vernon: penis."

"Um."

"It's okay Vernon, just answer whatever you're thinking."

"Um."

"I know you're having some problems being open Vernon, but just think of the thing we've discussed most in the past weeks and I think you'll find you're answer."

Vernon actually didn't have any specific thoughts to go with the word "penis"; although he was starting to have a few specific thoughts about Dr. Nash.

"Um, Rita?" Vernon responded.

"No, no, Vernon," smiled Dr. Nash. "I know you're trying your best, but I think there's something else that we've spoken a lot about you building and working on, don't you?"

"Um, plate rack?"

Dr. Nash giggled with wild abandon and triumphantly made a couple of marks on his note pad. He was whispering all sorts of congratulatory praise to himself regarding his astute observations and keen patient insight. Vernon wondered what kind of shop teacher Dr. Nash had in school. A birdhouse probably would send him over the edge, Vernon thought. Dr. Nash should probably start with a penholder instead.

Vernon was escorted back to his room where he continued

marveling at what was either a streak of ivory or very light beige on the floor tile. Before he could settle which color it was, the head nurse came in holding a bag with his name on it. She smiled widely and handed it to Vernon along with another bag full of medicine bottles.

"Congratulations Vernon, Dr. Nash says you can go home now. Here are your clothes and your medicine. We have a schedule in the medicine bag that tells you when to take what pills. We've called a cab and they'll be here to pick you up in a few minutes to take you to your apartment."

Vernon was dazed, but nodded dutifully. He looked around the room. The only possessions he had were half a dozen "Get Well Soon" cards that Rita had sent with long rambling letters that he had never fully read. Vernon changed into his clothes and then nurse escorted him outside the building. Vernon had "forgotten" his cards from Rita on the dresser. He had also forgotten the pills and his schedule of appointments with Dr. Nash in the wastebasket by the main entrance.

Vernon gave the cab driver the directions and drifted off into a hazy sleep full of birdhouses and plate racks.

Doc and Purvis wanted to drift off to sleep. Instead they were both hiding underneath Elise's bed, with two round faces grinning at them. Renee was reaching a pudgy arm underneath the bed trying to grab one of the dogs' collars. Carson just tried to coax them out with a dog treat cooing "Here puppies. Come and get a yummy."

Doc and Purvis huddled against the far wall, as far away from the dog biscuit and the fleshy hand waiting for them.

After Carson had tried to mount and ride Doc like a horse and Renee had try to get Purvis to wear a dress, both dogs skulked around in the shadows, fearing the next endeavor of their tormentors. It was almost relieving when Elise chased her siblings out of the room and forced Doc and Purvis to go for another hellish run.

The dogs followed Elise grudgingly as she jogged mile after mile listening to her Margaux Maddux seminar tapes. Just when Doc and Purvis thought she had decided to rest long enough for them to relieve themselves, she'd start in again. Doc and Purvis began to think that wearing dresses wouldn't have been that bad. Luckily, fate intervened.

Elise was tying her shoelace at a park bench and preparing to use her positivity to drag Doc and Purvis at least another mile, when Haddock Leeson appeared. Haddock was a big, beautiful blue-eyed, barrel-chested exchange student who was so naive and dumb that he simply radiated positivity. Elise was in love with him and couldn't wait to tell him about the cute boy she had met last summer that she got to write pretty songs for her. She couldn't remember his name at the moment, but that wouldn't detract from the story, she thought.

As Elise showed off too much leg and brushed her ample chest against the big foreigner Doc and Purvis whined quietly. Elise, not wanting to miss a single broken and simple-minded phrase that Haddock uttered, quickly unfettered the dogs and left them to take care of their business.

Doc and Purvis dutifully relieved themselves and trotted back to Elise. Elise didn't notice their return; she was too busy giggling too loudly at Haddock's repeated and incredibly bad attempts at clever banter. With each mishandled pun or bungled cultural reference Elise would laugh as if it had been executed flawlessly and then would show off her legs or brush up against Haddock. Doc and Purvis waited for her to finish, but just when it seemed she had flaunted and teased enough, she would begin anew.

Doc and Purvis flopped down by the bench and waited for Elise for an hour. If you put that in dog hours, they were waiting seven hours for Elise to finish with her witless prey. Finally, Doc slowly rose and sauntered off into the nearby park. Purvis was momentarily torn until he caught a whiff of perfume and bubblegum, then he too rose and followed Doc.

And somewhere, Wayne and Yvonne had sex again.

V

Dr. Nash was nodding supportively as Rita screamed at him.

"What do you mean you just discharged him? Christ, you'd think someone would let me know. He's probably out with some sort of machine gun waiting to kill me! Is that what you want?"

Dr. Nash kept nodding with a contemplative frown of concern on his face. After a pause he cleared his throat quietly.

"I felt, in my professional judgment, that Vernon had reached a point where he would be best suited by returning to the community with regular visits with me. After all, he never actually hurt anyone; there are no legal charges pending at this point. Vernon made a breakthrough in our in-patient sessions that I felt warranted his status to be re-evaluated.

"He's been very cooperative with all the goals of therapy and I thought that it would be in his best interests to return to a less structured environment. I was just looking out for what was best for Vernon. I think that's the best way to approach this situation, don't you?"

Rita's face was crimson with rage as she glared at Dr. Nash across the desk. She was about to begin shouting again when she stopped and smiled sweetly.

"I guess that's fine doctor, if that's your professional opinion. You've had more experience in these matters, anyway," she leered.

Dr. Nash was suspicious of the sudden change of her demeanor, but continued. "I'm glad we agree, Rita. I think our ultimate goal should be to help Vernon regain his life as much as possible."

Rita nodded enthusiastically. "By the way, Dr. Nash, since it was a professional decision to allow Vernon to discharge early, you and the hospital are liable for him, right?"

Dr. Nash paused, "Well, liability is determined mainly on the basis of negligence in such cases—for instance if the doctor discharged a patient when he knew or should have known that the individual was a risk—"

"So, say a patient who has a history of making violent

threats is released and then, instead of going to his new home, goes to his old house—terrorizing the new occupants before disappearing without a trace. Would the releasing doctor be responsible for the emotional trauma of the new occupants or the trail of bodies that such a patient would undoubtedly leave in his wake?" Rita asked sweetly.

"Um," replied Dr. Nash.

Vernon hadn't actually "terrorized" Wayne and Yvonne. In his medicated state he wandered into his old house and promptly tripped over Wayne and Yvonne who were in the middle of a coital engagement on the floor of the enclosed porch. Vernon was unsure what to say, so he just shrugged and advised Wayne to "keep up the good work," and then he shuffled off to the kitchen to make himself a cheese sandwich.

Yvonne went screaming into the street and Wayne sat in the porch undecided if he should join in his wife's expression of terror in the street or just lock the door from the house to the porch and wait for the authorities to arrive. Kurt and Courtney distastefully pranced around Vernon's feet as he rummaged through the refrigerator, hoping to show their contempt of this new intruder through their haughtiness. Vernon just nudged them out of the way with his foot as he sorted through the exotic cheeses that Wayne and Yvonne stocked their fridge with.

Vernon sighed. This obviously wasn't going to work. All they had was some sort of all-natural, hand ground multigrain bread and a variety of block cheeses he couldn't even pronounce. Vernon wanted the individually wrapped cheese facsimile that he was used to.

Vernon wanted his house back. He wanted his dogs back, too. The two fluffy bundles of venom hissing and parading around his feet were poor substitutes for Doc and Purvis, and they weren't his, anyway. Of course, all this raised the slightly disconcerting question of who they belonged to and why they now lived in his house.

Vernon thought about going back to the hospital, but he wasn't sure he had any other woodworking stories that could equal the excitement and intrigue that his plate rack had caused. Vernon grabbed an apple out of the fridge and sauntered out the back door. He headed down the alley to the enclosed bus stop at the corner of the block. He sat back on the bench and took a bite of the apple and waited.

After everything he had been through, there was one person glad to see Vernon although Vernon didn't know it. Sitting next to him in the enclosure was the broken and rancid corpse gurgling happily. The ghost had made it to the end of the block before he had lost all sense of direction and ended up in the bus stop. The ghost had been forced to endure countless strangers invading his new shelter, unfriendly dogs following his scent and growling menacingly at him and several juvenile delinquents and drunks urinating on his shed.

After all indignities he had suffered as a result of the hated Wayne and Yvonne, the ghost was relieved to see Vernon shuffle to his bus stop. If Vernon was still around Doc and Purvis certainly had to still be around somewhere. Vernon took another bite of the apple and sighed as two police cruisers flew by, sirens blaring and lights giving off intermittently blinding flashes of white and red.

Wayne and Yvonne were explaining the situation to the officer. Yvonne was wailing about she could never feel safe in her own home again. Wayne was trying to explain why neither of them had any clothes on when the police arrived. The phone rang and Yvonne managed to get herself together enough to answer it.

"Hello?"

"Is this Yvonne?" came the monotone reply.

"This is Yvonne," she answered, stifling a sob.

"Hi, how are you today?"

"Not so good. Some crazy man just broke into our house and threatened us."

"That sounds horrible."

"It's very upsetting. I should call my parents and let them know we're alright."

"Your parents? Do they live nearby?"

"No, they're in Michigan. Who is this?"

"You know, if you want to call them at significant savings we have a calling plan that can suit your needs."

"What?!?"

"At International Telecom we're always expanding our

services to better suit your needs as a consumer. During this special introductory offer I can offer you 500 free long distance minutes and only six cents a minute after that. There's only a low monthly fee of $6.95 for this great value."

Leonard heard the phone line go dead. He sighed and waited for the machine to dial another number. He was getting used to people hanging up on him. He took another swig of the tepid bitter coffee from his mug and began to play with multi-colored tacks that marked the only divergence from beige in his cubicle. The phone uttered two short beeps indicating Leonard was once again about to attempt to sell someone something they didn't need.

Janice used to always say "time and tide wait for no man." Vernon would just smile and nod when she said that and then she would top off his coffee. Vernon thought that time and tide might not wait, but he would have to; the next bus wouldn't be coming by for another half hour. He took another bite of the apple as the ghost waited patiently next to him.

It began to drizzle lightly but Vernon didn't really notice. He was wondering where he could find a good cheese sandwich and maybe a cup of soup. He thought about going to the cafe where Janice worked. It made sense, after all—she would give him free coffee and Vernon was in love with her. Vernon took another bite of the apple and just decided to wait for the next bus. Being in love seemed like a lot of work for a rainy day without Doc and Purvis and no house.

The ghost didn't have a house, either, or Doc and Purvis.

The ghost realized that he had taken the bus before. The ghost didn't usually spend much time reminiscing—aside from the dull throbbing and sudden numbness in his legs during that night in 1964. That didn't really count as reminiscing, the ghost decided. The ghost was getting little flashes of memories from his life before his death. He remembered waiting at the bus stop—it had changed to be sure, but it had near where the current one stood. He remembered waiting with a sack lunch and a forest green metal thermos. Nothing else in particular, just waiting with his lunch and a thermos.

And somewhere Doc and Purvis sprawled out underneath a tree and wondered if they would ever get their dinner.

The Midnight Ride of the Chalupa Ponies and Ten Questions for a Dead Man

I

You are the reader

I am the writer

This is the story, or at least an introduction of sorts to it.

This is Vernon. Vernon is on a bus going heaven knows where. We've met Vernon before so I won't beleaguer the point by mentioning his dogs or his ex-wife.

Next to Vernon is the ghost. The ghost doesn't know what to do on the bus. I would suspect most ghosts don't use public transportation, so that's understandable. The ghost got frustrated thinking about riding on buses and started thinking about his thermos. It was a good thermos that always kept his coffee hot. But the ghost doesn't have it. Dead people don't drink coffee.

This is Leonard. He used to be called Spook. Whichever name he uses, Leonard is basically a loser. But that's okay; there are more losers in this world than any other group. Leonard tries to sell long distance service or low-interest credit cards over the phone and nobody likes him—especially the people he tries to sell long distance phone service or low-interest credit cards to. That also means Leonard doesn't like his job because, while being a loser, Leonard is not a militant loser. As such he does not enjoy actively proving he is a loser on a daily basis to wide cross-section of the populace. If he did, that would make him a politician or a sports commentator.

There are a few other folks you should probably know by now. There's Elise who is not a loser, but is nonetheless a moron. Then there's Rita, who is Vernon's ex-wife and essentially pure evil, or at least that's what Dr. Nash thinks.

Dr. Nash is the doctor who likes plate racks. He was Vernon's doctor when Vernon was committed. He doesn't like Rita one little bit, but he's still afraid of her, like Vernon used to be; so they have that in common, at least.

Wayne and Yvonne are the happily procreating yuppie couple that drove the ghost out of his home and onto a bus sitting next to Vernon. The ghost thinks that they are pure evil, which might garner an objection from Dr Nash, but the ghost had lived with Rita too, so might be a better judge in either case.

This is Doc. Doc likes chewing things.

This is Purvis. Purvis likes chewing things, too.

Doc and Purvis don't like Elise or her siblings Carson and Renee, but they don't think they're pure evil. They don't have much use for thinking of pure evil. They do have a use for rancid meat, but all that's already been covered.

I am the writer, as has already been established. I am probably a loser too, but that's outside this story's scope.

You are the reader. You might be a loser, but I don't know

and I'm not really one to judge, anyway.

This is the story, or at least the end of an introduction to it.

II

Life was best thought of as an individual's struggle against the great inhuman tide of capitalism and mediocrity, Leonard philosophized to himself. He sat back in his chair with his special headset on listening to a Mr. Walter Diller say a number of nasty things about Leonard, the horse he rode in on and Leonard's mother. Mr. Diller hadn't met Leonard's mother and Leonard didn't even own a horse. Leonard flipped a pencil nonchalantly through his fingers as Mr. Diller continued to express his thoughts on Leonard.

Leonard had asked him if he had wanted the new Monolith Bank credit card with a 0% APR when Mr. Diller had told him to do something uncouth to himself. Leonard responded that with such a low interest rate, Mr. Diller could easily pay someone to do that for him, and since Mr. Diller was such a valued customer, he would also receive frequent flyer miles for doing it.

Mr. Diller apparently was not much of a plane person because he told Leonard he could take the frequent flyer miles and put them somewhere unpleasant. Leonard pointed out that he was miles away from Mr. Diller and that, to insert the frequent flyer miles, it would make much more sense to use the new Monolith Platinum card to both save an instant 15% on his airfare as well as racking up an additional 5000 flyer miles to either make his return flight with, or just to have on hand for additional inserting.

It was about this time that Leonard began contemplating

the ramifications of free will in a cold, indifferent, Godless corporate universe. Meanwhile a class full of trainees was giggling hysterically as their instructor feverishly tried to disconnect from monitoring the call while simultaneously trying to find out what extension was on the call.

When Mr. Diller finally hung up on Leonard, Leonard decided to wander around and get a fresh cup of the complimentary sludge they called coffee. As he ambled his way to the break room, Brad, Leonard's supervisor, caught up with him.

"Hey, Leonard, the team is doing some restructuring right now, so you're being transferred to Kevin's team. You're on the same account, but they're moving you to the other side of the building. Is that alright, buddy?"

Whenever Brad asked Leonard if something was alright, it meant that there really was no other option. Leonard had overheard Brad talking to the account manager, Karen, and she would ask if it was alright if his team was restocked with a number of disappointments and underachievers and it was pretty much the same thing. If anyone would raise an objection to either Brad or Karen, or anyone, really, they would be told that they were sorry and it was really out of their hands. Orders had come down from corporate dictating every specific change and that, if there was a problem you'd have to talk to either their supervisor, a human resources person or another account manager, each of which would refer you to their supervisor, a human resources person or another account manager.

Leonard actually liked jumping around from team to team. He knew he'd always end up on Brad's team anyway because his numbers would be so poor. Each time he would make up a new name for himself. He would create little games to play while on the phone. Sometimes he would make up an accent. Other times he would call sobbing hysterically or omitting parts of speech. "No Verb Day" was a favorite. He had scheduled "No Preposition Day" and "No Gerund Day" based on the success of "No Verb Day."

Leonard decided his name would be Chet while he was on Kevin's team. He gathered his colored wall tacks and the few papers he had at his desk and made his way to other end of the building. As he was leaving, his replacement, a dour looking man of about fifty was already setting up in the cubicle. He arranged his pencils and pens immaculately and stacked his papers neatly in the corner of the desk. Leonard wondered how long the new inhabitant of his desk actually expected to last.

Leonard made his way to the other wing of the building where he was met by a bright-eyed man of about thirty wearing khaki pants and a sweater holding a complimentary Monolith Bank coffee mug. "Hey, are you Leonard?"

Leonard looked him over. He had already been on Kevin's group twice and each time it was the same. "No, sorry. I'm Chet; I was transferred from Carol's group. You should have gotten a memo."

Kevin looked puzzled for a moment. "I don't remember anything about a Chet. It doesn't matter; I'll just put you in the cubicle we were saving for Leonard. If he shows up I'll just put him in a new cubicle. Seems like they do this to me every couple of weeks. They send me a memo telling me someone from Brad's group is coming and then they send me someone else. It's lame, man."

Leonard nodded sympathetically. "Yeah, corporate can be real pricks sometimes. It's amazing that anything gets done."

Kevin grinned widely, "Amen to that. Listen Chet, if there's anything you need, just swing by my cubicle, I'll get you set up. Alright buddy?"

Leonard nodded and shuffled down the carpeted aisle to his new corporate dungeon. "No Gerund Day" sounded like a good way to start off in Kevin's group.

Doc and Purvis didn't much care about gerunds. They weren't fond of any part of speech aside from a few specific nouns like "dinnertime" or "outside." They both would have liked to have heard "dinnertime" at that moment. The sky had begun to darken with clouds and it was time to eat.

Doc and Purvis had sat in the cover of the brush and watched people run around and play for most of the day. They had even watched Elise buzz around frantically calling their names with poor Haddock Leeson in tow. Haddock had even tried to help, but his cries sounded more like "Dook" and "Pourvees." Elise gave up after a half hour when it started raining and convinced Haddock to walk her home to console her anxiety and grief over the missing dogs.

Doc and Purvis finally ambled out of their cover at twilight.

Neither was particularly sure how to proceed. They wandered the area, poking through garbage cans and sniffing various foul-smelling puddles. Doc wandered into the street and was promptly killed by a bus. Purvis was alarmed briefly until Doc's ghost, which smelled wonderfully rancid, appeared and ambled back to him.

Doc really didn't feel like moving towards the great tunnel of light and decided instead to rejoin Purvis to find the ghost, or at least Vernon. Somewhere in the back of Doc's dead mind, he knew which way it was to the ghost. Purvis just followed Doc along because that's what he always did. That and Doc now smelled very good.

"There is no end that isn't a beginning." At least that's what Margaux Maddux, who for her part was experiencing the "end" part of the equation, had said. Margaux had no doubt fluttered up to heaven the first chance she got, or better yet, fluttered up to heaven just to be tossed back down, the ghost thought. The ghost really didn't want to go to heaven, but he still resented the fact that Margaux Maddux would have been offered the afterlife the same as he had. Margaux Maddux had money, fame and popularity to sustain her in life—it would just figure that she wouldn't even had to have waited in line to get to heaven. All the ghost had in life was his thermos. It was a damn fine thermos at that, but still he suspected even Margaux Maddux with her deluded dreams of a better life through positivity would impress the folks in the afterlife. It was probably just another big popularity contest, anyway.

The ghost was sitting on another bus with Vernon. Vernon had decided to take a vacation and bought a ticket for the bus to Omaha. Vernon really hadn't wanted to go to

Omaha, but that's where people seemed to go for vacations, so Vernon thought it was worth another try. The ghost was sitting next to him; silently fuming about the injustices of the world and the afterlife as a small child repeatedly kicked the back of his chair.

Vernon wondered what Doc and Purvis were doing. He had no way of knowing that Doc had been escorted off the mortal coil by the mid-town line. Vernon began to wonder absent-mindedly if his life was supposed to be a metaphor some larger universal truth. The best he could figure was that his life was a cautionary tale against either cheerleaders or woodworking.

Vernon wondered if he should be on the lookout for woodworking cheerleaders as he drifted off to sleep and dreamed about a group of angry cheerleaders with bandsaws chasing Herbie the flying wallaby.

III

Elise had a dream. She was standing in a green field full of butterflies and daisies. That wasn't unusual. Where most people dream of falling or being in high school and realizing they were naked, Elise usually dreamed of idyllic settings or fluffy, floppy-eared bunny rabbits. She even once dreamed of a flying wallaby. This dream was different because Doc was there. Elise suddenly realized that poor Doc was dead.

Elise began to feel very un-positive, but then Margaux Maddux herself appeared glowing with radiant light and a holy aura. Elise then realized two things: Doc was in a better place where Margaux herself was looking out for him and Elise had to make a pilgrimage. Elise awoke excited and full of fervor. While she had missed her chance to see Margaux alive and well in Tampa, she would begin a trek to visit her final resting place. It would be her trip to Graceland or Jim Morrison's grave, except much happier and probably considerably more tasteful.

Elise immediately began packing her bags. Elise decided that she would travel the humble path like pilgrims and monks of old, so she only packed two suitcases and a small duffle bag filled with 40 Steps to a Happier You! as well as all the seminar tapes she could get to fit. She then sat on her bed scribbling enthusiastically in her journal waiting for sunrise so she could finish her preparations.

Vernon hadn't made any preparations. He felt hot and sticky and was pretty sure he smelled bad, but he didn't much care. He was on vacation and this is what people on vacation did. Vernon decided that it was time for him to assert his fundamental averageness. He vaguely considered buying a pair of shorts to complete his "on vacation" look.

Vernon checked his pocket. He had $236 and some spare change left. He wasn't sure how far that would get him in Omaha, let alone whether it would get him back. It didn't much matter, he reasoned. It wasn't as if he had a job, a home or his dogs. He really didn't have anything, except for this vacation.

Life didn't strike Vernon as particularly complicated anymore. There were the Vernon's and the Elise's of the world. There were things to be owned and things that seemed to own you. There were jobs and mortgages and low-interest credit cards and, if you were lucky, a couple of dogs. Other than that, everything seemed pretty blasé and arbitrary. You could get married, or not. You could buy a house or not. You could have kids or not. There were a lot of options available, but none of them struck Vernon as naturally superior to their alternatives.

Granted, he wouldn't have someone to look after him in his old age, or someone to carry on his name. Then again, he never had to cancel plans to watch sick kids nor did he have to sit through interminable games of soccer or PTA meetings. All else being equal, Vernon felt like he was ahead of the game. Of course, he still hadn't finished that plate rack. But then again, he didn't have any plates to rack anymore either.

Vernon sighed. Perhaps he was missing the point of the plate rack. The list had been as close as he had come to finishing anything of importance. He had finished college, but that seemed to be more of a formality than an actual "life milestone" contrary to what the over-permed, over-painted speaker at commencement had insisted.

He figured that this was some sort of mid-life crisis. Rita had her own views on the subject, but she hadn't even had the good sense to buy her own plate rack. Vernon didn't know what a mid-life crisis really meant. He hadn't found a young nubile trophy wife to replace the one that he had been so wonderfully dissatisfied with. He hadn't purchased a motorcycle or a sports car. He hadn't begun painting or sculpting or anything remotely artistic to explore who he was.

He just felt like he was riding on a train and that he could see just ahead where the tracks ended. Instead of jumping off the train to some sort of great unknown freedom, he had just sat back and hoped that as the train flew off rails he would either have the good fortune to die quickly or the train would suddenly decide that it no longer wanted to be a train. After all, look what being a train had gotten it, in the middle of the air with no tracks and little more than certain and unpleasant destruction waiting. So instead of a train, it could discover that it was actually an automobile and would continue on after a brief sigh of relief. Of course he was unsure if trains could want to be anything else. Vernon for his part really didn't want to be anything else, but he wasn't precisely sure what he was to begin with, so that really didn't help.

The ghost knew what he was, insomuch that he knew he wasn't alive anymore. Being a ghost was pretty simple, actually. Aside from being dead, there were really no expectations. Sure there were the "go-getters" that would rattle chains or appear in dark hallways as some sort of mist, but they were just out for attention. Regular dead folk would either go on to whatever was next or, like the ghost, just be dead. There were no mortgage payments, nothing to own, and the bonus was that even-tempered dogs seemed to think dead things were pretty neat.

The ghost had tired of the constant jostling in his seat at the hands of the tiny oppressor behind him kicking the seat so he had begun wandering around the bus. He eventually settled next to a middle-aged woman who was sleeping by the window. In her lap was one of those innocuous and ubiquitous women's magazines. The page loudly proclaimed "Are you happy? 10 Questions that could change your life!"

The ghost settled in next to her and began to read.

IV

Leonard was staging a corporate coup-de-tat. Of course Leonard didn't know that he was doing anything that day aside from avoiding gerunds.

In a rare act of pity the usually petty and cruel corporate gods decided to bolster Brad's horrendous numbers. They assigned James L. Curtis, a quietly ambitious bookish middle-aged man who could sell long-distance and dish out low-interest credit cards like there was no tomorrow, to Brad's team.

No sooner than James L. Curtis arrived, he was overheard by a class of trainees to caustically insult a customer—a Mr. Walter Diller to be specific. Of course, the corporate gods were enraged and quickly removed Mr. Curtis from his position for his conduct—which he stringently denied even after his firing. There were two immediate results of this action. The first was that Brad, the lowly and bedraggled team manager was demoted immediately as was his supervisor and his supervisor's supervisor (and a human resources person, just for good measure). The second was that a bright up-and-comer named Chet was named site manager. Although no one could track his exact numbers down, word was that his numbers were very good and that he had been reassigned by corporate to Kevin's team for the sole purpose of salvaging the account as well as serving as the eyes and ears for corporate.

Kevin was the first to march up to Leonard to give him the good news.

"Good news, Chet. You've been named site manager. I

just got the memo from corporate. Seems like you've been on their radar for quite some time."

Leonard nodded. He had known about the memo. He had dreaded the memo. His workstation computer had been accidentally given administrative access a few weeks before. Leonard had played around with all sorts of settings and bells and whistles. But his crowning achievement was creating the Topeka, Kansas corporate consulting office of which Chet was the manager.

Leonard had begun simply enough by recommending that every cubicle be fully stocked with an array of brightly colored wall tacks. He had thought nothing more of it, until, a week later, every cubicle had a little clear plastic box full of multi-colored tacks.

While Leonard was far from the brightest member of the company, he realized that his fake memo and the appearance of the tacks were too closely connected to be a coincidence. Soon Leonard was sending out memos to have the break room snack machine stocked with only treats that met with his approval. Without fail, the vending machine was adjusted to the wishes of the corporate consulting offices. Leonard realized that he could not make changes too specific to his own position for fear of being caught. With that realization the momentary thrill of his new found power was lost.

The memos from the Topeka branch became more infrequent, but they didn't disappear all together. Leonard scheduled a mandatory "Amnesty Day" for the company where employees could admit the days they had left early or account for the pens they had stolen and the like without fear of reprisal. It hadn't been the success he had hoped for, but Leonard still enjoyed hearing the confessions of his co-workers either wracked with guilt for having a friend punch them out after they left early or the sly proclamations by the unrepentant of success at the company's expense.

What Leonard couldn't have expected and didn't even know about was his newfound hero status. Rumors and whispers of James L. Curtis—the man who defied corporate—were spreading like wildfire. They started innocently enough with a group of trainees quietly talking about what they had overheard in class. Soon other stories surfaced about "No Verb Days" and false names. Some even said that James L. Curtis had managed to stay in the company or patch into their phone lines and still took calls. The seeds of a revolution had been planted and their battle cry was the name of the unemployed dour looking man of about fifty, "James L. Curtis."

Leonard didn't want to take over the site. Some corporate paper-pusher desperately wanted to ingratiate himself to the mysterious manager of the Topeka consulting site and had ordered and then pushed through a proposal that Chet be given a ridiculous raise and total control of the entire call center. Leonard desperately tried to call off the reassignment and raise, but the heads of corporate would hear of no such thing. Mistaking his legitimate desire to have nothing to do with the company as a subtle and sly way of requesting higher salary and perks the company kept him at the center and gave him a free hand over any and every aspect of operations and, to top it off, a personal assistant of his choosing that started at junior executive level pay.

Leonard resigned himself that he would be the unwitting head of the call center. At that point Leonard realized that only an incredible fool would reveal the ruse to the blind, deaf and dumb corporate figureheads. Months could go by with someone gone and if there wasn't a corresponding document, memo or mission statement indicating it was true, then for all intents and purposes they were busily slaving away at their cubicle, even if they were, for example, dead.

The first official move that Chet made was to appoint a little known and under-achieving phone tech named Leonard as his personal assistant. Leonard shrewdly decided that he would have to be around the office anyway because a few people actually knew him as Leonard while the rest feared him as the administrative near-deity that was Chet. With Leonard acting the role of the personal assistant, he could be either or both, depending on the situation.

Leonard quickly packed up what few items he had and made his way to the luxurious corner office reserved for the site manager. In the small office leading into the main office Leonard arranged his things, which consisted of a notebook, a couple of pens and his box of tacks. On the desk in the inner office was a memo from corporate expressing their collective joy that Chet had accepted the position and detailing the allowances he was given to decorate his office, moving expenses, travel expenses, housing expenses, medical, dental and vision benefits (all of which were exorbitant by any measure) as well as his corporate ID card that allowed him access to various box seats, finer restaurants, first-class travel arrangements and hookers (although the latter wasn't implicitly stated, but the available pictures and listed "services" of the escorts left little to the imagination).

The second official move by Leonard was to suggest that the ingratiating paper-pusher be reassigned to the non-existent Tulsa development center and await further instructions, at his own expense, of course. And finally Leonard ordered pizza for the entire site and then took a nap under his huge oak desk.

Wayne received some excellent news that day. He had long toiled at the best way to make an impression on his supervisors. After months of bootlicking at work and optimism at home things finally seemed to be going the right way. Yvonne's endless nagging had abated when she learned Wayne's seed had finally met the stringent standards of her womb and succeeded in accomplishing something other than the completion of two minutes of frantic and unrewarding physical exertion and uncomfortable positions. Wayne found himself left increasingly to his own ends with Yvonne doting on various details. While he knew he should feel excluded, he felt more a sense of quiet relief.

At work he had learned of a then-unknown corporate hotshot and saw his opening. He flooded his supervisor, his supervisor's supervisor and countless human resources people suggesting, pleading and insinuating that the mysterious up-and-comer be given a site of his very own to manage. It was a stroke of genius to suggest his own site as the benefactor. Of course he also e-mailed Chet to gain his trust and good favor.

Ah, Chet, what a robust and strong name, Wayne thought

to himself. In his mind he pictured that Chet was a kind of Adonis in khaki—brazen in his defiance of convention, bronzed and powerful with a set jaw and one of those cool looking stainless-steel coffee mugs. Wayne was so smitten with Chet that he began absent-mindedly writing press releases and brief thank-you speeches for Chet and himself. Had Yvonne found his affections so completely devoted to another she would have left him in a second right after taking him for everything he was worth. Fortunately Yvonne was busy with preparations for herself and the baby—all of which had nothing to do with Wayne.

Wayne wasn't able to contain his gasping cough of joy and adulation when the official memorandum was circulated by corporate stating the Chet would be arriving—better yet had secretly been in their midst for a number of days—and would be assuming control of the site immediately. Wayne straightened out his cubicle and rehearsed his greetings and congratulations when he and Chet were finally face-to-face.

The moment never came, but in its place a brief and succinct message from Chet arrived on his computer screen. Wayne was being reassigned to a hush-hush development group in Tulsa as a program supervisor. It was his big chance and he could hardly wait. He quickly composed a gushing reply to the e-mail and hurried home to Yvonne. He was finally becoming his own man, he thought as he proudly marched up the steps of the house. He called out to Yvonne to tell her the good news and was promptly hit in the face by a flying block of unpronounceable cheese. As the throbbing in his nose and forehead subsided enough for him to open his eyes he looked up at his wife who stood over him, furiously gathering more cheese into her arms.

V

"In life we all run into many obstacles and 'opportunities.' I say opportunities because that's what most of life's frustrations really are: opportunities for us to grow and change. It's very easy to fall into negative thinking and frustration when things don't seem to work out the way we want them to, but we must always remember that these difficulties are life's way of making us better people.

"I've written books, appeared on television and done countless numbers of speaking engagements and I'm always amazed by the people I meet. Each one has their own special and beautiful story about how they've used their opportunities to be better husbands, wives, mothers, fathers, doctors, lawyers and most importantly human beings. I've listened to their personal stories of triumph and perseverance and I began to notice particular thoughts and ideas that seemed to keep recurring.

"I go into more depth in my book, but here are ten questions that will help you more clearly analyze your own process of 'person building' and how to get what you really want in life.

"Question #1: looking back, when were you the happiest?"

The ghost gurgled thoughtfully for a moment. He reflected on his childhood. He remembered all the misadventures he and his brother Wally had together. He remembered how his mother was always doting on the two of them while miraculously maintaining the house. Their father always been somewhat distant, but always was available. The ghost could remember many times he and Wally had been able to count on their father's sagely advice to guide them through the twists and turns that life brought.

Then there was Wally's wormy friend, Eddy. The ghost hadn't thought too much of him, but still, even in his ingratiating way, he—

Wait. That was "Leave it to Beaver." Damn.

"Question #2: what obstacles do you see preventing you from happiness now?"

The ghost pondered for a moment. Wayne and Yvonne definitely had to be considered, but in all fairness the ghost wasn't really all that happy before they had arrived. Of course the transition from mildly irritated or apathetic to miserable was progression in the wrong direction. The ghost thought maybe his best bet was in working backward.

Get his house back. Get rid of Wayne and Yvonne. Get Vernon, Doc and Purvis back. Get Rita back. Wait, that was going too far.

Maybe if he just got his thermos back, that would be enough.

"Question #3: what steps are you taking to be happy now?"

Well, the ghost had moved seats. Not having that kid kicking his seat helped him. Sitting in a different seat didn't really make him happier, though. It just kept his level of discomfort to a minimum. Was that the same as happiness?

The question probably meant that the ghost should be finding some way to get his thermos back. But he didn't have much use for a thermos. Dead people didn't drink coffee, even if they really wanted to.

"Question #4: what opportunities do you have right now for happiness that you may not have taken advantage of?"

The ghost was pretty sure that riding on the bus was not an opportunity for happiness. Even though his own flesh was grey and rotting and his stomach was bloated with his misshapen facial features from the Louisville Slugger that had shattered his skull, the ghost could tell the smell was atrocious. Vernon, for his part, was as ripe as anyone on the bus having gone a number of days without bathing.

The ghost sighed and looked around the bus. The occupants were either mostly senile or looked like they were either on the lam or trying to get to the next Grateful Dead show. Happiness wouldn't be spending the rest of eternity hanging out in a bus. In fact, had Wayne, Yvonne and Rita been on board it would have been as close to hell as the ghost could have imagined.

The ghost didn't belong to the "happiness in the journey" camp. He would have just as soon stayed in his house— without Wayne and Yvonne—and just spent his afterlife in relative peace. In retrospect, the ghost wasn't even sure what he was doing on the bus. He had hoped to follow Vernon to wherever Doc and Purvis were, just to regroup. Instead he had dragged his broken putrescent form up the brief stairway onto a Greyhound bound for Omaha where he didn't expect to get any closer to anything resembling a resolution.

"Question #5: do you feel that, given the opportunity, you could make others understand you and appreciate your uniqueness, thereby attaining a sense of peace about your own life and purpose in the broader scheme of things?"

No.

"Question #6: if you could talk to yourself 5, 10, or even 20 years ago, what would you tell your younger self?"

It's not worth the wait. Of course, the ghost was still dead twenty years ago in either case, so the point was pretty much moot

"Question #7: do you consider yourself to be always looking forward to the positive or always reflecting on what's already taken place?"

Well, there was the reliving of his death, but that wasn't really reflecting. It was more just a way to pass the time when he was bored, or when people were having sex with no consideration to those around them. The strange thing was that each time he noticed something a little different— a new detail or sensation he hadn't noticed before. It was strangely poetic actually—the initial explosion of pain on his temple and then the alternating bright lights and blackness that seemed to accompany each new blow. The blurry forms of his assailants, and the strange tastes, sounds and colors that washed over him as his brain started to hemorrhage.

The ghost had never been one to look too far ahead. Even when he wasn't dead and was just a guy with a green thermos thinking about the future really never interested him. It seemed that the only hope the future held was that life would find a more creative way to attack, usurp and undo him.

The ghost didn't feel persecuted. He just believed that there were two general camps in life: the Vernon's who were around to be walked on, used, ignored and discarded and the Rita's and Elise's of the world who did the walking, using, ignoring and discarding. It was a very efficient system—supply and demand. There would always be a need for people who would take abuse, clean toilets, say "yes, dear" and turn the other cheek. It could never be a one-to-one ratio because the Rita's and Elise's were temperamental and petty and would always need a slightly different variety of person to step on to get where they were going. It was the natural order.

What was more, the ghost saw no problem with it. There was a certain peace that came from a life lived in quiet bored agitation. There was little doubt that the Elise's of the world had no clue about the world they inhabited and the Rita's were just as likely to be chewed up and spit out. Like the ghost had always said before he was the ghost "The only problem with being the big fish in a little pond is you have watch where you shit."

VI

Leonard was having a rare day. It had occurred to him that the call center hold music sucked. He had made the mistake of calling asking for Chet in a paranoid attempt to show that he was not Chet. In retrospect he should have known that the workings of the corporate machine were indifferent to such trivial details. As long as Chet wasn't shown to not exist, all would be fine with the world. All the rest was frosting.

In either case, Leonard was forced to listen to a collection of lesser-dance hits from 1982 performed by the elevator music orchestra until he finally could take no more and hung up. The next day he marched into the call operations room and slammed down the Chalupa Ponies demo tape and said in his most pompous, authoritative Chet-like voice that the tape was to be used for all company hold and promotional music and from then on all other music selections would have to be approved through his office.

A few days passed and Leonard had forgotten all about it until Chet started getting memos and customer service notes about the music. When he first saw the memos he figured he was found out. Instead, the notes and memos were all in favor of the music change. Again Chet was the golden boy of the organization, but the highlight was yet to come. At the very bottom of the pile were a number of requests from college radio stations, lesser talent scouts and even a couple of girls seeking more information on the band.

Yeah, The 'Ponies had groupies. Now he was definitely getting some tail, he figured. As he sat back in his chair, or Chet's chair—he couldn't remember which belonged to who—the courier guy knocked. He came in with a next-day envelope. The courier held out a pen and a receipt with a red 'x' on it. Leonard scribbled a random wavering line across the paper feigning a signature and then took the envelope. The courier smiled and gave his trademark half-wave before disappearing down the hall to hit on the receptionist some more.

Leonard opened the envelope and out fell airline tickets and a registration form. Leonard was becoming accustomed to getting random packages of perks and quasi-bribes, but this looked different than the usual corporate offering. Upon rechecking the address label it simply said "Hold Music Band."

As Leonard delved into the packet, he could hardly believe what he was reading. It was an all-expense paid trip for the Chalupa Ponies to play main stage at the inaugural night of the "Greater Omaha Alternative Big Rawk Show!" which featured at least a decent sampling of bands Leonard had actually heard of. Leonard quickly filled out the registration form until he got to the portion requesting information on the band members, equipment needs and general biographical information.

Should he invite Chad and Luis? He was even tempted to invite that little prick Corey Burton just so he could make fun of him and kick him out of the band in front a bunch of hot groupies backstage. Of course he would still have to listen to him jawing about "his art" and "deeper meaning through inward examination" and all his usual bullshit that only talked about when girls were around. Maybe he could set it up so he would be in first class with all the hot flight attendants while Chad and Luis were in coach. They could put Corey Burton in a dog kennel in cargo. That would be pretty sweet.

No. It was time for Leonard to become Spook again and take the helm of his creation. Spook was the Chalupa Ponies. Were the Chalupa Ponies. Was the Chalupa Ponies? Dammit.

As for equipment, Leonard had no idea what he needed. All he needed for open mic night was his acoustic guitar (he had been banned for life from using his electric guitar and amp in the coffee shop) and if he was going it alone that might be the best route again. After all, just playing an electric guitar with no one backing seemed kinda desperate and while Leonard was clearly desperate he had no deep psychological need to convey the sense of urgency his bladder and stomach impressed upon him to anyone else, especially an entire festival crowd of anyone elses.

Leonard just wrote "using acoustic guitar—outfit accordingly." It sounded official and confident. Either way it would have to do for now.

It's important to point out here that, in some great twist of karma, universal fairness or grace, depending on your worldview every loser seems to be given at least one chance to change his or her status. Perhaps it's just the law of averages. The ghost didn't like averages, but was more than happy to go along with them as long as they didn't kick him into another tax bracket—at least while he was still alive. But dead people don't pay taxes.

The ghost for his part probably had his opportunities. It didn't much matter to him. It didn't seem that either position was inherently any better than any of the others. The ghost couldn't remember anything other than his thermos and thought that regardless of how he had been in life he would still only remember a thermos now. That all life ended up being was a fuzzy memory of a forest-green steel thermos—people just weren't in a position to know that until it was too late.

Had that been a question? Question #8 had asked about what mattered most in life. The ghost tried to retrace his steps from life and thermoses to what mattered, but in the end he wasn't able to come up with anything better.

Leonard was also working on some philosophical questions, but they had to do with his own biography. He had struggled between using his real name, using only Spook or Spook in quotation marks between his first and last name. He settled on just using Spook, but he was unable to think of anything that reflected a larger belief or that sounded cool. Cool lines got the chicks. It had to be one line, too, because chicks need to be knocked out with one killer line or else they just think of you like a brother. Being a brother sucked.

In frustration Leonard just threw the application in its return envelope with only "Spook is" as the biographical statement. It was trite, but Chet had a late lunch at the aspiring sushi bar that all the aspiring corporate types went to so that they could use their company expense accounts.

Leonard slipped on the suit jacket he had ordered for such functions, slicked his hair back and prepared to be at least 20 minutes late, which ironically took no less than 45 minutes to do.

VII

The distance to Omaha had dropped to double digits according to the big green highway signs. Vernon barely moved during the entire trip aside from a quick restroom break during one of the stops. Even when the kid had switched seats with his mother and began kicking

Vernon's chair, Vernon barely stirred. He had learned to zone out long periods of time over the years. For instance, he didn't remember anything between his 4th anniversary to Rita's birthday—he had hoped they had been in the same calendar year, but couldn't swear to it.

The ghost marveled at Vernon's ability to simply continue for no other reason than that was the direction he had been set in. Of course the ghost was riding on a bus going through a quiz in a woman's magazine for no other reason than he had boarded with Vernon. The ghost decided not to think about it anymore.

"Question #9: are you willing to change if you're given the opportunity?"

And then it struck the ghost. This was a test to see if you were an Elise. The ghost would have felt sick to his stomach if that part of his brain that controlled such urges hadn't been flipped across the dark basement by the claw of a hammer. Change was not a dynamic thing, it was an either/or. The ghost felt horribly betrayed by the magazine and the firm, lithe model/actress on the cover whose smile seemed to encourage trust in the bold words that encapsulated her body.

There were two types of people in the world, and as if the Rita's preying on the Vernon's of the world wasn't enough, they were trying to recruit other Vernon's to prey on the Vernon's left behind. It was cannibalism.

"Question #10—Pick up Margaux Maddux's latest book, <u>40 Steps to a Happier You!</u> for more information on these steps as well as the tenth question that help you attain everything you've been missing!"

The ghost bubbled hatred and venom. Even in death the accursed peddler of bullshit was inescapable. Something had to been done—something more than going to a bus stop.

Meanwhile Purvis and the ghost of Doc were on a freight train. Purvis had followed a hobo who had taken the dog under his protection on the rails. Purvis followed him because he smelled like the ghost, not because he was dead, but because he really needed a shower. Ghostly Doc had been wary at first, but eventually followed Purvis' lead and the two flopped down in the car with the hobo as the train began to lurch and heave forward. The hobo shared a can of beans with Purvis who ate it hastily as Doc tried unsuccessfully to nudge his way to the food with his incorporeal form. Doc wasn't hungry, but he had always had first rights to anything. Doc let out an irritated little growl and then flopped down in the corner where he was soon joined by Purvis.

There were a number of destinations, but the hobo was en route to Omaha to meet up with some old friends. As Doc and Purvis lay patiently in the train car neither of them had a clue that they were heading towards a confluence of forces and worlds that had all diverged that quiet night they had waited in the basement, the smell of varnish still thick in the air, for someone to fill their bowls and call "Dinnertime!"

An Aside

I

This story is not about Vernon. It's not about Leonard or Chet or Spook or whatever he's going by now, either. It's not about Elise, Wayne, Yvonne, the ghost, Rita, or even Purvis or the late Doc. This story is about a man named Pascal Deneut.

Pascal insisted that people call him Wade, although there didn't appear to be a reason to call him that. Even so, Pascal was very insistent that he should be called Wade and aside from his doctor and the head nurse, everyone followed his wishes, as will I.

In case you haven't gathered, I am the writer. You are the reader, etc. etc. If you have any questions about your role in this story refer to the previous chapters or see a psychologist—they love people like you. People like you pay for their children's braces, but that's another topic for another time.

Wade was very old. He'd been in the St. Jude Nursing Home longer than anyone. Wade couldn't walk anymore and spent most of his days waiting to be wheeled around by the pretty nurse who always had something she would rather do than wheel Wade around the Nursing Home. Wade always wished he were younger so he could bone the pretty nurse, but he was sure that even if he was boning her, she would have something else she would rather be doing. She was a lot like his ex-wife who was probably dead, too.

Wade had been keeping an extensive list of people he had known that were dead, or he suspected were dead. There was only one person on his list he was absolutely sure about, but he didn't talk about it with anyone. Instead he would sit in the community room in his wheel chair waiting for the pretty nurse to either give him food or wheel him back to his room. While he waited he made mental notes of the people he saw and figured out when they would die. He had an uncanny ability to determine when a fellow resident was going to die—usually within 72 hours. Most of them didn't have long. There was already one lady in a coma. She was as good as dead and really couldn't count for much except a warm-up. The old man with colostomy bag would go first, probably in the next couple of weeks. After that it would the grandmotherly woman who was always making quilts for the staff and the other residents. And after that Wade was willing to say that the nursing home administrator would show up all his elders by either committing suicide or keeling over from a massive heart attack. Either way, Wade would outlive them all.

Wade had stopped making friends a while back. He knew he was going to survive them all. After burying a few folks he had become acquainted with, he decided the whole thing was a gargantuan waste of time and preferred to spend the rest of his days watching other people die. For the longest time Wade himself had preferred to not die, but lately he had begun to rethink his position.

Granted, Wade's idea of "making friends" was probably a bit divergent from the common definition. Wade just wanted people to laugh and nod knowingly at his dirty jokes, believe all his lies and loan him money without question. He really never had a deep interest in what they had to say and if one of them seemed to be heading a conversation, Wade took it to be a sign that he needed to tell another story about a clandestine rendezvous with a hooker or how he'd like to bone the pretty nurse.

People had become a blur as they had rushed past him in a head-on charge into death. No sooner than one had been packed snugly in the ground another would be clamoring for his spot in the great soil condo timeshare. Wade was nonplussed by the whole process, but still the routine was becoming tedious.

Wade always remembered the stoic, romanticized view of old age and old people that others tried to impress upon him growing up. Officially being old now, Wade saw nothing noble, wise or otherwise endearing about the whole mess. It's hard to consider anything noble or stoic when it has to wear diapers because it shits itself. He didn't know any sagely kind old men or doting sweet old ladies. Everything at the home smelled faintly of piss and most of the residents, while putting on brave faces, really couldn't tell you where they were, why they were there, who was president or why in God's name they should have any desire to participate in a group craft time that consisted of gluing popsicle sticks together to make little cabins.

Wade spent many hours each day planning his death. The trick was to make his passing the centerpiece of the St Jude Nursing Home. He didn't want one of those straggler funerals where one or two of the residents showed up along with a bored orderly with a couple of the senile patients. Only slightly better was the kind where everyone showed up and all the women cried and the old men would shake their heads and say "it's a shame; really makes you think about what's important."

The funeral that Wade wanted was something so jarring that only the bravest and sturdiest of souls would make an appearance. The other residents would talk in hushed whispers at mealtime, each afraid to mention it by name and then quickly retreat to their rooms with fear and trembling at the horror that had befallen their fallen comrade. Those were the funerals that were legend. Those funerals turned schmoes into people who were immortalized—to be forever called in melancholy reverence by the first name. Even years later the staff would be unable to formulate words to express what had happened. And if there were any surviving residents that weren't completely senile, their faces would grow solemn and their voices would tremble with a low hollow resonance that most closely resembled religious fervor.

Yup, that was the kind of funeral Wade wanted and it would take no small amount of planning on his part for it to come together. The most basic concern was timing. If you were the second, third, or God forbid forth person to pass in a row, you just wouldn't have the same momentum that the first one did. Of course being the first one didn't make much difference if you were going to have three or four others tagging along on your heels, either. Then it would just be remembered as a "rough stretch" and the impact would be nullified. There were degrees of consideration to all of those general rules as well.

For example, you needed a warm-up death. Some old biddy who had been in a coma for a month or two that people still remembered, but who wasn't in close quarters any longer was ideal. A few people would be broken up by it, but for the most part it would just make most people a little moody. The blue-hair down the hall had been taken to the hospital two weeks and had developed pneumonia while in a coma. She hadn't been around too long anyway and she would probably do just fine.

The second step was to develop a stoic and fatalistic attitude that indicated something horrible was in the works. This was imperative because without a sense of dread in the populace there's no sympathetic pre-emptive response. It added an element of mystery to the whole affair and without fail the overactive morbid imaginations of the infirm always projected new layers of horror and suffering that surpassed the human capacity of endurance.

It could never be spoken of, even indirectly. The trick was making sure everyone saw a brave stiff upper lip without making it obvious that said lip was being displayed. Always quick to believe the worst—especially after so many of their friends and neighbors had been carted off by the medical examiner—the groundwork would be set with minimal work on Wade's part.

Of course there would have to be some payoff to the suspense built up. After sowing the belief of horrible imminent death it would be unacceptable to choke to death on a tater tot. If one could manage to get an "undetermined" cause of death it would be striking the mother lode. Better yet if some organ was hugely swollen to the point it horrified medical personnel or was missing altogether. There had to be some defining characteristic to make it sensational.

That would be a bit of a trick, but Wade didn't think it was going to be insurmountable. He had already begun setting the whispers in motion about some incurable heart problem he'd had since the war. Wade wasn't in the war. He had been serving time in a chain gang in Mississippi for selling stolen methadone to unwitting high school kids. Local law enforcement wasn't impressed and the next thing Wade knew he was working ditches while everyone else he had known was being sent to be shot at or bombed by the Japs or the Krauts.

Even so, Wade was more than happy to tell everyone that he had been knee-deep in the shit and blood in Saipan or at Eisenhower's side crossing the Rhine. When asked if Patton wasn't the one who crossed the Rhine Wade would just call them Commie faggots and then ask them what they were doing while he was protecting freedom and liberty alongside his friends who were being blown to bits by the Axis hordes.

People began to hold him with a quiet awe with each outburst of apparent righteous indignation. It was important to build and maintain the proper image: a healthy dose of stodgy benevolence mixed with defiant fatalism. He could feel the curiosity growing among the residents as the pretty nurse wheeled him around indifferently to his corner of the community area. Some of them thought he was brave. Some thought he was strong. Others thought he was serene and at peace with his fate. Wade thought he'd really like to nail the pretty nurse in the broom closet.

II

The list began: dad, mom, granddaddy (x2), grandma (also x2), the guy with polio who used to live next door, that guy Bert from the bar...

Wade had been compiling the list as long as he had remembered. In his days at St. Jude the list had grown with veracity—each entry, most a vague reference ("funny-smelling guy who ate all the pudding," "fat woman with the cat," "old homo down the hall," etc...) catalogued another person that Wade was pretty sure was dead. Wade didn't take such things for granted and wouldn't say definitively that any of them was dead, but Wade was satisfied for the purpose of the list that they were more or less worm food.

Wade couldn't remember why he had started the list. Some of the early entries written in a schoolboy scrawl included Abraham Lincoln, George Washington, Virginia Rappe and Callipso—the neighbor's pet parrot. Eventually it became more organized, if less personal, with dates, even approximate times when available. Most just had a name or description and a date with occasional arrows indicating changes in chronological order.

In 1964 there was an entry that was scratched out with the phrase "see other list" written in parenthesis next to it.

1964 had been a good year. Statistically, Wade had his best year in 1964—bedding no less than 100 women (mostly hookers) that year and only catching the clap once. It had started with a bang with the gleeful divorce from his wife who, for all her faults had actually managed to contain Wade's skirt chasing for eighteen grueling months.

While his lecherous womanizing had offered no impediment during their courtship, as soon as the marriage ceremony had finished he had found himself the target of his new wife's radical plan to rebuild him into an actual husband. Suddenly Wade found himself being forced out of bed hours before noon. With a kind of deviously twisted mechanical efficiency Wade would find himself sitting in an uncomfortable high-backed wooden pew every Sunday morning at his wife's side even after a night of fierce drinking and debauchery.

Adding insult to injury, he was expected to bathe and shave regularly and wear pants when simply sitting idly on the couch. Even worse, after he had performed his husbandly duties, he was assailed by an endless string of questions and petty anecdotes about life and love from his new wife.

Wade learned quickly that, unlike their relationship before the marriage, trying to give his wife cab fare to go somewhere else after the act would result only in emotional upheaval and bloodshed. She owned the former and he the latter.

If Wade had anything good to say about his married years, it was regarding his ability to move silently as well as lightning fast reflexes that allowed him to avoid being hit by most pieces of dining wear, small appliances and a wide array of foods—even if his back was turned when they were hurled. In spite of the benefits granted by his newfound skills, Wade decided that married life didn't suit him.

For as trying as the experience of matrimony was, attempting to end it turned out to be even more taxing. Initially Wade had thought simple infidelity would be sufficient to drive his plucky bride away. Lipstick on the collar and perfume on his clothes didn't even put a dent in her resolve. It did, however, manage to put a dent in the back of Wade's head.

One tumultuous night after his wife had found no less than two bar napkins with names and numbers scrawled on them and an empty prophylactic wrapper, Wade found himself agilely dodging plates, silverware and the occasional coaster. In the chaos he had failed to notice his wife slowly advancing on his position. As he turned his head, assuming that the barrage had stopped, he caught a glimpse of his wife bearing down in silent fury with a cast iron skillet in one hand and a rolling pin in the other. Wade chose the rolling pin.

As he sat in the emergency room with the intern stitching up the back of his head, Wade wondered if there was anything he could do to save himself. In a fit of desperation, Wade left the hospital and headed directly to nearest tavern. After several drinks, Wade secured the services of a fake blonde with a beer gut who was no less than 40, but she swore she was a 19 year old co-ed who had only been with her high school sweetheart shortly before he was sent to die in the service of his country.

Wade didn't much care if she was 19 or 40 or 100. He just knew $20 would get him a tumble and hopefully either an ex-wife or the sweet release of death. He took her home, knowing full well his wife would be returning shortly and set to violating his rental on the kitchen floor.

Wade heard his wife's footsteps coming up the landing and to the door. Wade bit his lower lip in grim anticipation and began feverishly pumping away at the bored 40-year-old co-ed beneath him. Noticing his quickened pace, Wade's indifferent recipient gave a few token moans and words of encouragement in hopes that she'd be able to get a couple quickies in before last call. Wade saw the door open and out of the corner of his eye, he saw her dark silhouette in the doorway. Wade closed his eyes tightly half expecting the sweaty, clammy skin beneath him was going to be the last thing he experienced on this Earth.

After nothing happened, Wade opened his eyes to see his wife quietly slipping down the hallway. He let out a sigh of relief and grinned widely. The hooker sighed and muttered "Alright stud, time to get off the pony unless you want to pay for another ride." No sooner than Wade had unceremoniously tossed her semi-clothed out into the hallway and slammed the door, he flopped down on the bed and slept like a baby for the first time in months.

He awoke the next morning only slightly hung over. His head still throbbed a bit from the beating he had taken, but it was still minor compared to the weight that had been lifted from his shoulders. He rolled out of bed and headed to the kitchen.

To his surprise she was there, quietly and dutifully cooking breakfast. She looked at him emotionlessly as he sat at the table. Wade wasn't sure what to do—after all, he thought he had seen the last of her. She quietly scooped him a helping of eggs from a pan and then poured him some coffee.

Perhaps he had given up on the marriage thing too soon, he mused. After all, if he could still chase tail unimpeded and she would come in the morning and make breakfast and clean up after him, why couldn't it work?

A warm breeze blew through an open window. Over the scent of bacon, eggs and toast, Wade smelled something burning. Curious Wade grabbed his coffee cup and looked out the window. In the middle of the street below, stacked neatly in a metal basin were all his girlie magazines, his favorite jacket, and the little book he kept the names and numbers of his conquests incinerated for all to see. Wade was horrified. If he had been a little less horrified he would have seen his wife coming up behind him. Wade received a matching dent in his head from the iron skillet.

As the world slowly came back into focus he felt someone grab his hair and pull his head up. Glaring down at him was the most fearsome incarnation of his wife he had ever looked upon. Suddenly there was a vice-like grip on his testicles and a slow agonizing twisting. As Wade whimpered pathetically he heard her hiss into his ear "If you ever even so much as think as bringing another filthy whore into my home, I will make you a eunuch, you stupid sorry sonuvabitch."

With that she gave a forceful twist and pull and the room went white with blinding pain. Marriage is for the shits, Wade thought to himself as he passed out again.

Over the course of the next few months Wade developed a reputation for being an instigator of bar fights that he never won. At least that's what the staff at the local emergency room was led to believe. Wade tried every last infidelity and con he could think of to drive his wife away, and with each attempt his beatings became more severe and unusual. Wade knew he had hit rock bottom when he was trying to explain to a second-year medical student that at Fallon's Tavern a young ruffian had started trouble and had proceeded to beat him with a soup ladle before smashing several bottles of perfume (which all young ruffians were carrying around for protection nowadays) over his head.

Wade had even tried to convince his wife that he was actually attracted to the effeminate bachelor in apartment 107. After a week of forced stolen glances and subtle innuendo, Wade was introduced to the bachelor's rosy fiancé. Wade was humiliated and broken. Almost overnight he stopped going to bars. When an attractive woman passed he didn't even raise his head to check out her backside. He found himself sitting glumly and listlessly in the harsh high-backed pews every Sunday morning for service, Wednesday nights for bingo and most Thursdays waiting for his wife to finish with her Ladies Aid meetings.

All the other women congratulated her on how her husband had turned his life around and now was becoming an ideal husband and a shining example for other men in the church. The other men looked at him sympathetically in passing, never making eye contact for long for fear that the same fate might await them.

The days all began to run together in one long unpleasant milquetoast haze. He would go to work, eat his lunch at noon, go back to work until five. At five he would make up an excuse to not join the boys at the bar for a drink and then make his way home where he was forced to sit and be attentive at the dinner table while trying to force himself to swallow the horribly bland noodles, corn and cream of mushroom soup that seemed to be the extent of his wife's cooking arsenal.

Soon the banality overtook him and he lost all concept of time. His days were differentiated only by his wife's social calendar. He found each task she delegated to him to be a rare joy that allowed him to escape his mundane regimen for a wholly different and new mundane regimen. Whenever she asked him to do something he would simply nod or answer "yes dear" timidly and set off to do it.

One day after returning from an errand to purchase a list of feminine products she had compiled for him he came to an empty apartment. There was a note on the kitchen table addressed to him. Wade looked at it for a moment before opening it. It said, in part:

You've let all the passion in our marriage bleed away. I try to make a nice home for us, but it's always got to be about you and what you want. I've wasted enough of my life trying to make you into a man Wade, but no more. I've found someone else who loves me and treats me the way I deserve to be treated. Someday you'll realize that I'm the best thing that ever happened to you, you sorry piece of shit! You'll be sitting here all alone and then you'll realize how much you love me and then it will be too late! Have a nice life.

P.S. You were a horrible lay.

Wade sat quietly at the kitchen table until the sun went down, wondering if he should reheat the left over noodle corn hotdish or wait to see if his wife would want to make something different.

The entry on the list for her had been written in bold, then crossed out, then rewritten and underlined and then had exclamation marks added, and then a couple question marks. Ultimately he just added a little star by the entry with the caption "Good Lord Willing" by it.

After the initial shock of finding himself alone again, Wade resolved never to be made the fool by anyone ever again. In January 1964 Wade resolved to make the coming year the kind of year he would talk about and reminisce over for the rest of his life.

III

Wade was talking and reminiscing to the pretty nurse who wasn't listening on his way to his weekly appointment. Once a week a doctor from the local mental health unit would come and visit with any residents that needed to see him or had been referred by staff. Wade had just started seeing him a couple weeks ago. To maintain the image of the tragic hero there had to be signs of mental strain. Of course Wade just talked about all the girls he nailed and his wild years when he went to see the doctor, but he still managed to elicit a mild sedative out him to make the whole process appear more solemn and official.

Dr. Nash let out a sigh when he saw the old man being wheeled down the hall. Ever since the debacle with Vernon, hospital administration felt it would be best if Dr. Nash was restricted to doing the hospital's pro bono work with clients who didn't have ex-wives who could sue the hospital for millions of dollars. Dr. Nash reluctantly took his assignment.

For the most part it was nice—mild delusions due to age and Alzheimer's, melancholy over watching family and friends dropping like flies around them, morbidity over their own impending end. All the ones who became a problem were quickly transferred to another facility designed to handle them. Dr. Nash didn't even have to take notes most of the time. He would just nod sympathetically and smile supportively and then write out a prescription for a mild sedative.

But then there was the file dedicated to Mr. Pascal "Wade" Deneut. Dr. Nash dreaded the hour-long marathons of misogyny, bigotry, perversion and debauchery. The first couple of session had been unpleasant, but functional. It was clear the Wade was trying to work some sort of angle with Dr. Nash, but Dr. Nash was actually interested in trying to dissect and diagnose the long list of pathologies that seemed spew forth unfettered from Wade's mouth every time he spoke a word.

With each new story, Dr. Nash was forced to endure countless sordid tales about sexual encounters that while most likely were completely untrue, still were told with such fervor and detail that Dr. Nash couldn't help but have a vivid mental image to accompany them. Dr. Nash had even upped the dosage and changed the scheduled time that Wade's sedative was to be given in hopes that he would be fast asleep whenever Dr. Nash made his weekly visit to St. Jude's. So far nothing had worked.

"Hey Doc, good to see you again," Wade cackled. Dr. Nash felt his heart sink as the pretty nurse who had wheeled him in disappeared down the hall, not to be seen again for at least another hour. Dr. Nash slouched in his chair, lowering his eyes so as to not directly interact with Wade and began doodling on his note pad.

"Doc, I gotta tell ya somethin' that's been botherin' me. No one else here knows this yet, but I'm dyin'."

Dr. Nash barely stifled a little squeal of delight. He saw Wade's eyes fixed upon him and so he faked a cough.

"That's very unfortunate, Mr. Deneut. What was the diagnosis?" Dr. Nash replied, hoping the quiver of joyous excitement wasn't apparent.

"Well, you know doctors—they don't tell you anything you need to know, but the long and the short of it is I only got a couple months left. I've bucked the odds so far, but I'm hitting the end of the line." Wade began matter-of-factly. "Doesn't matter to me. I've had a good life. In fact, just last week I nailed that nurse that wheels me around. Boy, oh boy was she a piece of ass, I tell ya."

Wade broke down into his trademark cackle that always accompanied one of his unlikely conquest stories. Dr. Nash was not to be distracted, however.

"This must be a very trying time for you, Mr. Deneut. Are you having problems sleeping? I can adjust your medication to help. I believe a healthy sleep schedule is one of the most important things you should be thinking about, don't you?"

Wade suddenly got very quiet and looked around the room suspiciously. "Okay, Doc, I need you to tell me the truth on something, alright?"

Dr. Nash nodded solemnly, trying in his head to figure out how many more sessions he would have to conduct with

Wade before he died.

"You guys are like priests, right? Whatever I tell you has to stay private and stuff, right?"

"Well, there is a privilege that generally keeps things—"

"Good, I got some stuff to tell you about this kid I knew a long time ago and you can't tell anyone until after I'm dead, you understand? No one else has ever heard this before, so it's important, okay?"

Wade was actually telling the truth—he had never told anyone about the story with the kid. It had been a long time and Wade really didn't feel some sort of pressing need to confess. The thing was that every great tragic story had to have a twist that set things in motion long before the story began. Wade knew that the nurses liked to listen in on the sessions with Dr. Nash and would chatter about them on their smoke breaks excitedly. Wade really was going to die soon, and it would be glorious.

IV

Wade had just called him "Kid." He liked the idea of having a sidekick named Kid and more to the point, Wade never really bothered to learn his name. Wade had met him at Fallon's Tavern a few months after his wife had left. Kid had a boy-ish face and sandy colored hair. He was a little smaller than average, but Wade saw him in a bar fight once and knew that he could take care of himself. The problem with Kid was that he was dumb. Astoundingly dumb, in fact. He didn't know when people were making fun of him and he didn't know when the odds were too far against him.

The night of the bar fight, Kid had taken on no less than twelve men at the same time—most of the men hadn't even instigated the fight, but were trying to restore the peace. In the initial confrontation with five drunken men Kid had dealt with them swiftly and mercilessly. Unfortunately when the other seven got involved to settle things down, Kid took after them with a devil's fury and received a sound beating for it.

Wade knew a good thing when he saw it. He knew Kid could be an effective deterrent against the various pimps and lowlifes whose ire Wade seemed to instinctively draw. After the fight Wade went into the alley where Kid had been unceremoniously dumped. He helped him back to his apartment and put him on the couch for the night. In the morning he found Kid still sleeping on the couch. Wade made them a breakfast of eggs, hashbrowns and beer and quickly earned Kid's eternal respect and devotion.

The reason Wade had managed to be so prolific in 1964 was that he was allowed to work without interruption. He could pursue any woman, stripper or whore without fear of reprisal. If a boyfriend, husband, pimp or other concerned party would take exception, Wade would simply set Kid on them and continue in his pursuit.

Kid for his part never asked for anything. He'd wait dutifully in the apartment hallway for Wade to finish with his endeavor and then Wade would unlock the door and Kid would just go lay down on the couch. All Wade would have to do was feed him breakfast in the morning and all was well. Wade would get off work and head to Fallon's and usually Kid would be there or would show up shortly after and the whole cycle would begin again.

Through the winter, spring and summer Wade was king of the universe. When he wanted pussy, he found a way to get some. When he wanted a beer, he drank some. He said what he wanted, when he wanted, to whomever he wanted and he was free of consequences. He was free of his ex-wife's oppressive grasp and determined never to be an object of contempt for anyone ever again.

Paranoia is the surest harvest from power and soon Wade was waist deep. He suspected that others were talking behind his back, plotting to get their revenge when Kid was away or making malicious comments about why Kid slept over at night. Wade knew what many of them were thinking and could conjecture what the rest might be. He even began to suspect Kid of secretly being aligned with his many enemies.

Occasionally when in a drunken fury Wade would start whipping Kid with a belt or anything else at hand. In the morning he was always apologetic. Even with his increasingly erratic behavior, Kid never raised his hand to Wade once, opting instead to let the inebriated man flail at him until his arms became too tired to swing anymore. Wade would always try and make some amends later on—a free drink or a hooker that Wade was finished with were often peace offerings.

Wade had been too hung over one morning to go to work. He finally peeled himself out of bed around four o'clock and got dressed and headed to Fallon's. On his way there he ran into Kid and they walked together. They were a few blocks away when a young couple walked by. They were whispering back and forth and the woman glanced over her shoulder at Wade and Kid and giggled quietly.

Wade flew into a rage, believing that he was the butt of their secret whispers. Without hesitation Wade sent Kid hurling at the man from behind, knocking him to the ground. As Kid straddled the poor man, beating him ferociously the woman began screaming. Wade's fury overflowed and he struck her hard across the face, knocking her to the ground leaving a large red mark. She continued to whimper in fear and pain and Wade continued to slap her.

Kid had finished with the man and stood watching Wade in shock as he attacked the girl. Wade stood over her as the anger subsided and felt oddly out of place. He looked at Kid's wide-eyed expression of disbelief and the whimpering man at his feet. He then looked down to the bloodied woman sobbing beneath him. A bus drove by and Wade saw a single face—it was a man shaking his head sadly as he clutched his briefcase and thermos looking right at Wade.

Wade suddenly felt flushed and a malevolent gnawing began in his gut. In all his years Wade had felt shame a few times, but never had been consumed by it. As the bus pulled away Wade memorized the face of the man and determined that that face would be punished for all the disdain, fear, hatred and guilt swirling around inside him.

As a light rain began to fall, Wade stormed down the street to Fallon's, leaving the scene behind him.

Over the next two months, Wade became fixated on the

man on the bus. He waited near where the attack had happened and watched for the bus studying each passenger intently hoping to see the man. He figured the man was coming back from work. Wade began staking out bus stops, trying to see which ones the man used. By the end of July, Wade knew where the man lived. On a cool night in August he brought Kid and made his move.

The house was unlocked and Wade and Kid quietly made their way inside. There was a quiet tuneless whistle coming from the basement. Wade took the lead and stealthily headed down the stairs. There was a single light bulb hanging down from the ceiling over a workbench. The man was sanding away at a piece of wood with his back to them. Wade felt the shame and guilt jolt through him again like a lightning strike when he realized it was the man from the bus in front of him.

Wade didn't have a plan when he and Kid had come in, but as they approached his turned back Wade felt only one impulse. He quietly lifted a hammer from the tool shelf and raised it over his head. The man cocked his head as if he had heard something and began to turn around when Wade brought the hammer down on the right side of his head. There was a sickening crunch sound and a dark warm jet of blood that arced gracefully across the room, disappearing into the darkness. Kid followed Wade's lead and began hitting the man with the baseball bat he had brought. A fresh spray of blood and tissue misted across the room in slow motion to Wade.

Wade let out a cry of indignant self-righteous vengeance before he turned the hammer around and began striking the man with the claw end of the hammer. After the first two blows little chunks of white and grey were flying around the room with each successive impact. The sound was a crackling followed by a squish followed by a little pop. The dull utility light swung back and forth from the ceiling casting playful caricatures and shadows across the unfinished walls.

Kid stopped hitting the man when he stopped moving, but Wade kept kicking the man in the face. With each blow Wade's anger only grew. It was unappeasable and hungry. Kid finally pulled Wade from the body. In a final show of defiance Wade grabbed the forest green thermos that had been next to the man on the workbench and hurled it at the limp mess of blood and mangled flesh. The thermos hit the body with a thud and bounced off, hitting the cement floor with a crackling noise as the glass liner broke.

Wade stood hunched over, wheezing as he desperately tried to catch his breath. A small stream of coffee was running out from the base of the thermos and mixing in uneasy swirls with the pool of blood collecting near the body. Wade felt no sense of accomplishment or relief, but he acted with spite and contempt in hopes that his actions would be able to convince what doubt he had that he was indeed avenged.

"Let's get the fuck out of here," Wade mumbled as he walked past Kid and up the stairs.

V

Wade finished his story with a half snort half chuckle and looked at Dr. Nash. Dr. Nash was sitting, eyes lowered to the ground, brow furrowed as if piecing together some perplexing puzzle. After a moment Dr. Nash shifted in his seat and looked Wade right in the eyes.

"So let me get this straight; you were given two months to live. So, with scheduled holidays and vacation that's, what, five or six more sessions? Am I understanding you correctly?"

"Thing is, doc, I'm real broke up about the whole thing with Kid, ya know? I mean when the cops showed up I told 'em that I heard him talkin' about killin' this guy and that I had nothing to do with it. I even got him to confess for Chrissake. I told him that I could get him out of it if he just said he did it all and that I would come visit him every week."

Dr. Nash let out a sigh. He wasn't as interested in the whole confessing past sins thing. He wanted to hear more about Wade being dead.

"I take it you didn't follow through on your promise?" Dr. Nash asked indifferently as he resumed his doodling.

"Hell no. I figured Kid would get wise to me eventually and that I'd come in one week to say a quick howdy and find myself being searched by some big guy with a real long glove. Just because I felt bad doesn't make me stupid. Christ. What kind of idiot would just walk into a scene like that?" Wade huffed.

"Well, why don't you tell him now that you're sorry?" asked Dr. Nash as he drew large breasts on his doodle woman.

"Couldn't even if I wanted to. Kid got the chair in 1969.

Never ratted me out, either. That was decent of him."

Dr. Nash kept sketching. "Well, have you thought about telling someone? Relatives might like to know that he was innocent."

"Naw. Kid didn't have any people. I did have this one thought, though. Why don't you tell me if you like it, okay doc? I've written out my will and it says in there everything I just told you, more or less. Anyways, since I got no family I was going to leave all my property to the children's hospital in his name."

Dr. Nash finished rounding out his doodle woman's curves and saw that Wade's time was almost up. "Well, whatever you decide I'm sure is fine, Mr. Deneut. I'm going to write up a new prescription for those pills I've had you on. I think a little more might help you sleep better."

Wade glanced out the window and saw one of the nurses creeping away down the corridor. "I think I've got everything I need, doc."

Everything to that point had been preparation and development for his plan. With his confession to Dr. Nash and subsequently, the entire nurses staff, the first domino had been toppled and they would all fall in sequence. As the pretty nurse rolled him back down the hall Wade watched the pieces fall into place.

The EMT's were just now removing the body of the colostomy bag guy from his room. Quilt lady had slipped into a coma at the hospital a couple days before. It was coming together rapidly now, but even Wade wasn't prepared for what happened the next day. As it was Wade was in his tragic hero mode.

Tragic hero mode was one of the final steps to solidify the belief in the myth he had wrapped himself in. By that evening residents knew of Wade's exploits in 1964 and that he had killed a man and let another man take the blame. A few of the men gave him indignant and angry looks. Negative emotions were key to the final stages. Only their ill will could fuel their final change of heart to something awe-inspiring.

Wade had been on his best behavior with the residents for the past week or two—which had immediately made most of them expect the worst. After every little statement he made about the future he would tack on "good Lord willing," and would say, "God bless you" with each little thing he was given whether it was the newspaper or the table salt. He acted grandfatherly to the visiting children and even managed to tear up once when a church group came by to sing hymns.

As the residents of St. Jude began shuffling off to bed the word came that the quilt lady had died. The time had come, Wade thought. The next day would be the day he stepped into his own little circle of history.

Accounts would differ greatly on many of the details, as they naturally would in such a situation, but they were all agreed on that it had started normally and quietly. Wade had been wheeled out to the community center by the pretty nurse. As she pushed him into a spot at the table he gently tapped her hand and said "God bless you dear," with a kindly smile that didn't reveal that he was thinking of boning her again in the broom closet.

Slowly, other residents walked in or were wheeled in by nurses. There wasn't much conversation about the quilt lady, mostly just glances thrown in Wade's direction and whispers about his mysterious past. Wade tried not to grin too widely as he overheard rumours about himself that were even more outrageous than the ones he had started. His favorite was that he was a fallen priest who had killed a man to save an orphan, but had been unable to forgive himself for having taken a life.

As Wade began gumming his cold, dry toast his heart skipped a beat. The Administrator walked into the community room wearing a powder-blue polyester tuxedo from the 70's complete with ruffles down the chest, wing-like lapels and a large matching floppy bow tie. It had been several years since the administrator had worn it and almost as many since he had fit in it properly. His gut hung over the waistline and the shirt's buttons were clearly about to give. But that wasn't the reason Wade was excited.

Panting heavily, faced flushed with flesh and hair sticking out where his clothes didn't fit or cover the administrator stood studying the room with two rifles strapped to his back. His eyes met Wade's and there was a moment of calm that washed over his face as he gave his stern smile and nod. Then he grabbed the rifle, lifted it above his head and screamed "Justice for all the goats! God bless all the goslings!" and fired off a round into the upright piano at the end of the room.

There was a scream and half the room hit the floor in a panic. Some scurried trying to find shelter from the madman. Wade sat looking as the carnage unfolded. The administrator was firing at random—not really at anyone and with his first six shots the total casualty list was the piano, a ceramic cat, two windows and two slugs landing in the spooky faux-marble statue of St. Jude in the corner.

Wade figured the administrator would either have a massive coronary or lose it all together, but this was unprecedented. The administrator began to reload has those left in the community room huddled under tables, behind furniture or anything else that was handy. After he finished reloading the administrator sat on the nearest table and cleared his throat.

"Now, ladies and gentleman, what have we learned today? I'd like to think that maybe we've seen what happens when you take advantage of something and it can't take anymore. I know you all know what I'm talking about—after all, how long did you really think that commercial emu industry would be able to continue its sinister mission with impunity? We all knew that this day would come when the emu, ostrich, rhea and all their flightless brethren would band together to stop this injustice. All of them but those fucking penguins—no sense of brotherhood from those polar sons of bitches is there?

"You'd think after years of working day in and day out for little or no compensation the penguins would be happy to fall in line, but no—too busy swimming like a bunch of fairies! I mean swimming! Swimming like a goddamn fish! Christ, even the platypus was marginally sympathetic with our plight and they're mammals, but not the penguin. Can't ruin the good image. Can't let anyone know that maybe everything is not okay with the marriage and that

Jimmy isn't in college—he's off in California starring in porn movies. Ostriches have problems, but you don't see them saying they need room to breathe or that they've grown apart, do you? It's all so fucking ridiculous and you try to explain to them that the problem is medical and the medical profession is working on a variety of solutions and that it's not that you don't love them anymore but they won't listen. They're probably already seeing someone else. Ungrateful black and white little shits!

"But God, you can't help but love them, even if they don't understand. I mean, let's face it, the emu haven't been as attentive as they could have been. When you're trying to put three ostriches through college on an administrator's salary you can't always spend your twentieth anniversary the way you had planned. It's not that you want to fly all of a sudden. Being constrained to land isn't so bad. Sometimes you just like to look through magazines of birds that fly and imagine a bit. But it's not like an emu suddenly wants to be with a finch or something…"

Each word hung in the air like an eternity. After the first hour the police had surrounded St. Jude's and had been yelling through a bullhorn. The administrator had never missed a beat, rambling incessantly of the plight of flightless birds in a world too concerned with receding hairlines, mortgage payments and unbridled penguin apathy. Wade hardly noticed that time was passing. He was seeing his wildest dreams come true and was patiently waiting for his turn.

It all happened suddenly. The windows seemed to explode and canisters spewing some sort of gas bounced throughout the room. The administrator was momentarily confused and a number of residents began to crawl, waddle or limp towards exits or adjoining rooms. Wade looked out the window and saw a ring of heavily armed police officers converging on the site with an army of cameras, reporters and on-lookers crowding closely behind. If it hadn't been for the nutjob a few months before threatening to kill those cheerleaders the turnout would have been maybe half of what it was today, Wade cackled to himself.

There was a shriek of terror and suddenly the pretty nurse who had been cowering unseen behind the quilting table came bolting out towards the exit. The administrator instinctively swung the rifle around at her and fired. It was if his entire life had waited for this moment. Wade saw him swing around with the rifle and somehow managed to get his old tired legs to work for the first time in almost ten years. He threw his body up behind the nurse as he saw the muzzle flash.

He felt an explosion inside his chest and suddenly felt a crushing weight against his body. As he fell to the ground he saw the administrator's face go white and mouth the words "God forgive me" before flipping the rifle around and firing one more round into his own head. As the administrator's body fell backward with an arc of blood flying sideways like a brightly colored flag Wade looked out the window to see every television camera in the world staring at him in shocked horror. He had done it. He had outlived them all and now there was only one thing left to do.

The pretty nurse was holding his head as he coughed and wheezed. She was crying and trying to tell him it was going to be alright. Wade looked up at her and then at the cameras and whispered "Tell Esther I'm sorry."

Even as Wade felt himself slipping towards the great light he saw hardened police veterans, jaded television producers and the pretty nurse who wanted to be somewhere else all looking at him with their hearts broken. That was the final thing to making a great funeral—a secret long-lost love. Of course Wade had never known anyone named Esther his entire life, it just seemed like a good name to use.

VI

The funeral was everything Wade had intended. The media came out in full force patiently watching the pretty young nurse tell everyone at the service how she had always loved and admired Wade like a father. Other staff got up and said how strong and brave he had been facing a terminal illness. A couple of the old veterans got up and spoke of how Wade had been a great patriot and soldier with Eisenhower's top-secret crossing of the Rhine before Patton.

The newspaper ran the story of Kid's innocence and how Wade had left his entire estate—which took an unexpected economic upturn with producers and executives fighting over every last article and item for their various special reports and television movies—to the local children's hospital in Kid's name. The final total was so high that it actually funded a new wing of the hospital which was dedicated as the Kid Memorial Children's Wing or the Children's Memorial Kid Wing—the hospital board was still trying to figure out which was less confusing.

Even years later the residents who weren't senile and the staff that were still around spoke of it in whispers, shaking their heads gravely and getting choked up as they remember the great sacrifice of Wade Deneut.

Meanwhile, in Hell, Wade was being subjected to heinous torture that involved a large stretching machine, his intestines and a two week old ham sandwich. Things had lost their spark lately so the head demon had introduced the sandwich in hopes of rejuvenating the spontaneity of their early torture sessions.

As the whistle blew for shift change, a group of demons came to Wade's horribly mutilated but still animate body. They were whispering excitedly to each other until finally one came up to him tentatively.

"Dude, you're him, aren't you? You're Pascal Deneut, right?" he chattered excitedly.

Wade flopped a piece of broken flesh as acknowledgement.

"Ah, dude, kick ass. I mean, seriously, this is totally an honor, man. You're a legend around here. I mean you were being eviscerated at the time, but everyone down here was glued to the tube for your funeral. It was totally fuckin' epic, man. I mean, you set it up, so you know what all happened, but man, it was just… just—"

"Epic," interrupted another demon who had slowly crept into the conversation from the group.

"Yeah, totally epic," agreed the first demon. "Oh, hey, I'm Troy by the way. Well, Troy Eater of Souls, technically, but you can totally call me Troy. This is Peanut."

"Hey," said the other demon with a half wave as he was

introduced.

There was a sudden booming voice over the intercom, the group behind them scattered instantly. "Troy, Eater of Souls and Peanut there is no fraternizing with the damned. If you're done please report to Supervisor Barry's office immediately."

"Aw shit, dude. We're totally busted. But look, it was cool to meet you—I'm a huge fan," said Troy as he started walking away.

Peanut just gave a nervous laugh before giving the machine another good half crank and setting the sandwich on fire.

"Sorry, just doing my job. Good funeral, though. Catch ya later."

Hell was for the shits, too, Wade decided.

Doesn't Much Matter

I

Me Tarzan.

You Jane.

Just kidding. I'm still the author.

You could be Jane, but I'm not one to presume.

Vernon, Doc, Purvis, ghost, Wayne, Yvonne, Spook, Rita and Dr. Nash, meet the reader.

Good to meet you. Would you care for a Ritz cracker with cheese? It's cheddar...

II

James L. Curtis. All of it had to be his doing. Wayne had heard the rumours, but all those things were small-time compared to this. James L. Curtis was the bitter old man who had made it his life's calling to single-handedly disrupt and antagonize Wayne's little world.

Wayne's eye was still black and blue from a block of cheese Yvonne had tried to meld with his brain by way of his eye socket a few days before. After months of bootlicking and ingratiating communications to any corporate mucky-muck with a phone extension or e-mail address Wayne had nothing to show for it. Yvonne was in the process of showing her displeasure regarding the situation when Wayne had managed to tell her of the Tulsa job between being pelted by various exotic cheeses.

Yvonne's wrath had been averted as she hurriedly began calling all of her friends to brag about their big promotion and all the doors that were being opened to them—even though Yvonne had little or nothing to do with it. Meanwhile, Wayne was left to take care of all the packing, moving and various intricacies and hassles of moving.

The response from Chet had been for Wayne to move as soon as possible to Tulsa and await further instructions. The project was so new and under the radar that staff were just being hired and the development center offices just getting furnished. It was to be Wayne's job to oversee this process and then take command of the center once it was functional. They had 72 hours to get to Tulsa and wait for follow-up directives.

When they had arrived in Tulsa Wayne had tried to call to center, but there was no listing. Surprised, Wayne had called the home office for contact information and was promptly put on hold. Over the next three hours Wayne was put on hold, transferred to countless other departments, subdivisions supervisors, supervisor's supervisors and human resources people. Finally Wayne decided to sleep on it. Chet had told him up to 72 hours, which gave them until the next day. Yvonne was already complaining about their hotel room as Wayne rolled over to go to sleep.

It had been expensive to get everything together on such short notice and Wayne and Yvonne were effectively broke. They managed to take out a bit of a loan on the house, which was enough to cover a month or two of mortgage payments and some minor expenses. Their only hope was that the job would start soon and the house would sell quickly.

Before Spook, or Leonard or Chet—depending on who you asked boarded the plane that morning everything was in place. He had arranged for the company to cover his travel expenses to the festival. Chet was sent to the festival to help sponsor and promote the event on behalf of some corporate off shoot development company called Chetsoft (that Leonard had created out of the non-existent Tulsa branch) in an attempt to lure the ever important 18-25 demographic. Meanwhile, Leonard had been assigned to go as his personal as Chet's personal assistant to mingle backstage with various artists to see if any of them would be willing to endorse the as-yet unspecified product that the non-existent spin-off company Chetsoft from the equally non-existent Tulsa branch had been in talks to develop. Corporate headquarters could have cared less what, if anything, was being developed by the non-existent firm and was in talks with a software developer to sell off it's remaining holdings in the company for $200 million.

Of course, once Chet and Leonard arrived in Omaha they would meet and escort a headlining musician for the Greater Omaha Alternative Big Rawk Show! representing the Chalupa Ponies in hopes of wooing him into a lucrative endorsement contract.   The preparations were rather intricate for the ruse. Spook spent most of the trip trying to figure out who he was supposed to be at any given moment. There were execs from corporate who wanted to pick Chet up at the airport for a power lunch. At six Leonard was supposed to be at the hotel to make appropriate arrangements at the hotel for himself, Chet and the Chalupa Ponies entourage and at nine Spook was supposed to do an interview at a local radio station. But before he left he had remembered to do one last thing.

Chet had reported the successful establishment of the Tulsa office, but since it had allowed Chetsoft to break off, the Tulsa office no longer served any developmental purpose. As such the Tulsa branch was to be reassigned within the company except for the site manager who had allowed Chetsoft to leave thereby rendering the Tulsa branch office useless. As a part of the new streamlining policy designed by Chet, any site manager who had no site to run immediately had their contract canceled and were released unconditionally from the company with no severance and a negative reference.

Leonard had assumed that his streamlining policy would have only a single target, but was surprised when he was notified that no less than 20 executive vice presidents, site managers and human resources people were immediately terminated within the company because they did absolutely nothing. The Board of Directors were so enthralled with Chet's brilliance to fire all those in the company who had no responsibilities that they immediately made Chet the Executive Vice President of Internal Affairs and Efficiency and gave themselves a raise from all the salaries they had just cut. The Board of Directors themselves didn't really do much, either, but since Chet was now an executive vice president he couldn't fire the Board without firing himself. They chuckled at their brilliance and collectively ordered another bottle of scotch.

When Wayne awoke the next morning he suddenly found himself unemployed and the scapegoat for the failure of the Tulsa branch. Yvonne was furious and although Wayne had done nothing during his twelve-hour tenure as manager for the Tulsa branch, Yvonne was already compiling a list of things he should have done to maintain his position and not disgrace his loving and trusting wife. As Yvonne began throwing hotel furniture at him, Wayne began to wonder how she had earned the adjectives "loving" and "trusting." Everything was so complicated and difficult, Wayne thought.

Vernon didn't think life was complex or difficult. Vernon just thought life was time consuming. Kind of like a long bus trip. Sometimes there was a kid kicking the back of your seat in life and sometimes it just smelled really bad. Sometimes you realized it was you that smelled really bad. In the end most of it didn't matter for much. If there were a Reader's Digest condensed version of life chances are there would be weeks, months, and even years that would be omitted just because nothing important happened.

Vernon watched as road signs and marquees advertising attractions, resellers and restaurants began to proudly proclaim that they were located in the heart of Omaha, just minutes away. Vernon vaguely realized that he had no idea what to do once he actually got to Omaha, but unfortunately at the same time he also vaguely realized that he would really like a piece of pie. Soon Vernon was thinking about pie.

Vernon liked pie. Apple, blueberry with whipped topping, sour cream raisin—millions of years of human learning, knowledge and ingenuity had managed its share of mass-murderers, genocides and atrocities, but it had also managed to take two layers of flaky crust and fill them with a seemingly unlimited number of tasty fillings that could quiet the soul and fill the stomach. Vernon didn't have much faith in humanity, but the fact they had stopped blowing things up and killing each other long enough to discover that pie was worth investing some time into said that at the very least their priorities weren't completely out of whack.

Vernon watched a plane touch down at the airport as the bus passed by. The huge metal machine coasted in and gracefully slowed to a stop. It reminded him of his dreams with Herbie the flying wallaby. Vernon wondered if Herbie could ever get sucked through a jet engine while he was soaring in the heavens. The thought troubled him, so he ate the bag of stale salted nuts that he had purchased from a vending machine at a run-down rest area the bus had pulled in to.

The plane jostled at the initial landing and then roared as it slowed. Elise could only think of how exciting all of it was. This was her pilgrimage. She had answered the call of heaven and was now ready to embark to the final resting place of Margaux Maddux. She scribbled her thoughts in her little pink journal.

"Today I become a woman. Or at least I act like one. When daddy said I could use his credit card to go to Omaha I realized that I'd finally found my own way. Of course the matching luggage set I had daddy buy is just adorable and while I was at the mall with him I saw this outfit that I just had to have for the day I go to visit Margaux.

"Everything is just so positive and beautiful and new. I mean, if even I didn't have a completely new wardrobe for the trip or first class tickets or reservations at the best hotel in Omaha, this would really be something deep and meaningful. I remember Margaux saying that she was happy when she was only making $50,000 a year as a junior public relations executive. She said that even though there were hard times making ends meet while pursuing her dreams, that she stayed positive and just believed that in life she was entitled to more than what she had. That was the most important thing—to always remember that there's always more to take from life if you want it badly enough!

"That's why I'm taking this trip. I know that there's so much more out there that I want and the only thing standing between me and my dreams is me. I've got to go out there and take it. I've got to be the one who asserts my positivity towards attaining my goals. Everything I could ever want is out there—I just can't be afraid to take advantage of all the opportunities life has in store for me."

Rita was taking advantage of her "life opportunities" by suing the hospital, Dr. Nash and anyone else not nailed down for releasing Vernon. She had sent Peter to dig for every last cent. The problem was, aside from the incident at the old house, Vernon really hadn't done anything. It was imperative that Vernon cause some more damage before he was captured so that any potential jury couldn't help but feel pity on his poor neglected ex-wife whose emotional well being and good name would be ruined by the reckless and irresponsible actions of a psychiatrist, his department, his hospital, a number of drug companies and the FDA.

Rita had managed to learn from relentless hassling and questioning of a patrolman that a man matching Vernon's description was seen boarding a bus to Omaha. Rita quickly gathered some things and jumped in her new sporty two-seater (courtesy of her and Peter's creative "reinvestment" with Vernon's house) and sped off to Omaha.

III

Omaha was established in 1854 by a ferry company servicing the Missouri River. Nestled between Iowa Territory and the newly designated Nebraska Territory it grew rapidly after being designated as the terminus for the Union Pacific's transcontinental railroad. In the ensuing years it had grown into a thriving city that harbored more than its share of insurance companies. Vernon had been in insurance and Omaha had always been a sort of work-related Mecca except with lots of older upper middle class white folks making the pilgrimage instead of devout followers of Mohammed. It was probably colder in the winter in Omaha, too.

Vernon was checking out various local landmarks and museums. He really wasn't all that interested in visiting museums and landmarks, but that's what his family had always done for vacations. Vernon remembered as a boy going to a natural history museum with his father. His father was just standing there, staring at a wooly mammoth puffing on a Lucky Strike. Vernon stood next to him holding steadfastly to his blue helium balloon staring at the mammoth.

Vernon's father sighed and flicked the ash from the end of his cigarette. "You see son, that's called a mammoth. It's sorta like a big elephant mixed with a camel far as I can tell. They're all dead now. Probably just as well. If there were still mammoths around then zoos would just get them instead of elephants and camels.

"That's all fine and dandy until you figure there'd just be a bunch of elephants and camels wandering around with nowhere to go. And pretty soon they'd find a way to put cows and horses out of work by doing their work for a fraction of the cost. That would just create hostility and tension and then there'd be some sort of war and they'd all be dead and the mammoths would be left with some survivor's guilt complex. I really can't see a brighter tomorrow with a bunch of melancholy mammoths meandering and mulling around. Doesn't much matter, though. I'm sure your mother will tell you something different about the whole stinkin' mess anyway."

Vernon's father took a long drag off the cigarette and let out another sigh as he mumbled "Goddamn mammoths."

Vernon continued on his walking tour of Omaha history. Omaha was proudly a leading manufacturer of corn flakes as well as the "800 number capital of the nation." It seemed to Vernon that there was a charmingly simple Zen-like order that summed up Omaha. The kind of balance that lets a place be the national toll-free capital and a huge producer of corn flakes—a simple, bland and nice place.

In 1863 they drug a body out of the Missouri river. A former judge and legislator from Kansas was found guilty for the crime and was hanged. At the execution it was a regular picnic with approximately 2000 people gathered for the event. The prisoner spoke to the crowd for about a half hour and seemed cheerful and unconcerned by most reports. After he finished there was a little ceremony and then he was executed. It was a perfectly pleasant social event and everyone went home happy, even, it seems, the dead man.

Vernon liked that idea—everyone was able to sit around civilly, enjoy their roast beef sandwiches and watch a man's neck being snapped—or maybe just suffocated to death. The placard didn't say exactly how he had died, just that he had been the first legal execution in Nebraska Territory. These days people didn't bond that way and if they showed up for an execution it wasn't to spend a pleasant afternoon with friends and neighbors to hear a speech, it was just to bathe morbidly in human suffering.

Vernon didn't much care for suffering. It was unnerving to watch. He never really paid much heed to his own—he had been married for a number of years after all—to Rita, no less. He was content to take it on the chin on occasion. Life was like that. Actually, Vernon figured life was a lot like a junior high schooler with his first crush—the fact life slapped you around, embarrassed you and pulled your hair just meant that life liked you, but was afraid to say something.

Elise didn't believe in suffering. She didn't believe in cancer in babies or that the good guy would die at the end of movies. It was all a bunch of negativity to acknowledge those things. Negativity was the cause of all horrible things. If negativity was forever banished from the world, Elise believed everyone would die old, plump and white. Or at least that was the image of the perfect world she had in her head.

Of course Margaux Maddux had died and died thin at that. She had only been white so the model broke down, but people like Margaux were special. People like Margaux meant so much that their deaths had to be special too. Those deaths turned very special positive people into people who were immortalized, to be forever called in melancholy reverence by their first name. Even years later those left behind would be unable to formulate words to express what had happened. And decades later, if there were any surviving friends or family members that weren't completely senile, their faces would grow solemn and their voices would tremble with a low hollow resonance that most closely resembled religious fervor.

Elise smiled to herself about how poetic that last thought had been. That thought was all hers and had never been thought before. She felt empowered at the realization.

Elise knew that this pilgrimage was the first step for her. She would be just as positive as Margaux Maddux and things would just end up alright if she persevered. She could give seminars and write books and give hope and inspiration to millions. She felt the conviction slowly well up inside her. It felt a lot like patriotism, except only to herself. There was something bigger and more important in life and it was going to be her. She glowed with resolve as the cab pulled up to the cemetery.

She stepped out of the car at the large gate and looked around for some sort of landmark. After wandering around some old wind-worn granite headstones she ran across a tall awkward pimply-faced groundskeeper. She smiled and showed off her legs and laughed too long at his jokes even brushed her chest up against him and soon she was being shown personally where the Maddux family plot was.

She approached the grave solemnly, clutching her airport bouquet of flowers. It was near the top of a slight hill, a huge marble edifice proudly and ornately proclaiming that it marked the final resting place of Margaux Maddux. There were fresh wreaths set up around it, some flowers, little cards and a few stuffed animals. In a neat little stack were several copies of <u>A Better Me, A Better You</u> and <u>40 Steps to a Happier You!</u> with little notes scrawled on the covers or loose letters folded inside to Margaux.

The only thing that kept it from being completely picturesque was an ugly simple grave marker sitting like a lump in the shadow of Margaux's. It simply read "MADDUX" in bland block letter and in the lower corners were the names "Joseph" and "Bernice." Bernice had two dates beneath her name.

Whoever they were, they should have had the good taste to take their tacky little marker and put it somewhere else. It was clearly mucking up the landscape for Margaux's shrine, Elise thought. Margaux deserved to have her own mausoleum complete with a little plague with her accomplishments on it and a place for others to share their thoughts and memories about her. And maybe a little gift shop next to it to buy memorabilia and paperbacks, too.

Elise decided she would never be tied down by the likes of some Bernice or Joseph. Elise suddenly realized that her destiny wasn't to be as good as Margaux; she was to surpass her. There would be no social climbers muscling in on her name. She would be a single solitary light to the multitudes in the darkness. The masses would cry her name asking for guidance and mercy. She could hear the chants of "Elise! Elise!" as she walked away from the grave. Her flowers sitting by the path where they were absent-mindedly dropped as she made her way to the great enlightened path of her destiny.

There's a side note to this part. Several hours later the ghost was lurching his way through the graveyard. Strangely enough, there really aren't that many ghosts in graveyards. Most of them consider it to be an afterlife version of a dentist's office. It's unpleasant to be at if you have business to do there and a non-consideration if you didn't. A few of the "over achievers" would do their little spooky things there from time to time, but even they often found cemeteries to be uncouth.

Aside from the occasional chirp of a cricket, everything was silent. The ghost had given up on Vernon after Vernon decided to spend over four hours investigating the indigenous species of Nebraskan conifers at the museum. The ghost quickly became lost and spent the rest of the daylight hours wandering through residential areas and being tormented by squirrels and the occasional stray cat.

The ghost was starting to become very sick of seeing things exist. The novelty had worn off shortly after he had been evicted from his porch and had gone rapidly downhill with each passing moment on the bus and in the museum with Vernon. Just when he thought that things had bottomed out he found himself looking up at a huge stone monstrosity.

Above him on a slight hill was Margaux Maddux's grave—the same accursed woman who had ruined his non-life through Elise and who had taunted him beyond the grave on the bus. It was a roller coaster short of being an amusement park, the ghost thought. There were balloons and cards and flowers all over every damn thing. The only thing missing (aside from the roller coaster) was some sort of tacky souvenir shop with snow globes, over priced paperbacks and some unnaturally perky twenty-something trying to hock coffee and collector's spoons.

The ghost saw the smaller gravestone dwarfed by Margaux's. Probably the original family plot done tastefully and befitting a family of modest and honest means, he thought. The ghost wasn't one to give into romantic notions of good honest hard-workin' folk. At the same time, anyone who had enough good humor and perspective to allow that God-awful thing to muck up their final resting place had to be given credit. It was kind of sad, really, that even in death the Maddux woman's desire to be omnipresent and influential was so great that a perfectly scenic little spot had to suffer a theme-park makeover.

The ghost gurgled to himself and then began wandering around again in hopes of finding something, anything really, that could get him home.

IV

The phone startled him when it rang. He fumbled around blindly for the receiver.

"This is Leonard," he mumbled.

"Good morning sir, this is the wake-up call for Mr. Chet—"

His eyes shot wide and he coughed a panicked phlegmy hack. "Um, this is Chet."

"I thought this was Leonard?" asked the female voice.

"Um, well, I'm his personal assistant. He's in the shower."

"He makes you stay in the same room with him?"

"Well, it's just easier that way," Leonard thought for a second. "But we're not gay or anything. I mean, you know, not that you'd think that. We just work hard... together... um, alone... But we're not gay."

There was an awkward silence. "That's good to hear, sir. I don't suppose you know about a Mr., um, Spook?"

"Why, what have you heard?"

"Nothing, there are just a number of messages here for him and some were saying that representatives from your company—"

"Oh, yes, of course. Yeah, he's in the shower."

"With Chet?"

"What? God no. We're not gay. Um, Chet just got out of the shower and then Spook hopped in because he was, um, just here all night, uh, hanging out. Cuz, you know, we're not gay or anything."

"Of course, sir."

"Um, so this is the wake up call?"

"Yes sir."

"Well, uh, good job. We're all awake. All awake in a totally heterosexual kind of way."

"Thank you sir."

"You think we're gay, don't you."

"Of course not, sir."

"You're very nice for saying that."

"You're welcome, sir."

"You're lying aren't you."

"Have a nice day, sir."

"I'm   not   gay."

"Good day, sir"

"I like women."

Click.

Leonard sighed. That could have gone better. As Leonard began his transformation into Spook and prepared for the Greater Omaha Alternative Big Rawk Show! it occurred to him that this could be a real turning point. Not one of those fake "real turning points" like high school graduation or marriage, but a definitive point he could look back at and say that that's where it had all begun. Of course he'd make allusions in interviews to his starving artist days and how he'd always been motivated, even if he'd only really been motivated to find a way to skip out on homework and nail hot chicks.

School was starting again soon. How punk would it be to drop out to do a full-blown Chalupa Ponies tour? Spook smiled to himself. He put on his ratty cut-off knee-high jeans and his ripped t-shirt with his dirty flannel grabbed his beaten guitar case and headed out. He threw on a pair of dark sunglasses as he approached the main lobby. Dark sunglasses showed that you were legitimate big time bad ass big shot. That and it helped him from making eye contact with the lady at the front desk who probably thought he was gay.

As Spook climbed into the charter limo he sighed. Unnecessary boredom was a rockstar thing. The mild contempt on his face for all things was definitely part of the Chalupa Ponies mystique. His carefully mangled hair was sure to score points with the chicks. Scoring points with (and eventually just scoring with) chicks was definitely his thing. And not a page of homework in sight. He was ready.

Elise was not having nearly as much success. After her epiphany in the graveyard, Elise had quickly mobilized to spread her gospel of positivity. She had managed to insinuate herself into a discussion panel at the university the night before titled "Feminism and the Myth of Progress: a Woman's Perspective for the 21st Century." Elise wasn't exactly sure what everyone else was talking about with their sexual politics and patriarchal oligarchies and class struggle in light of larger cultural gender norms but whenever she was called on or had an opportunity she would happily proclaim that the problem wasn't alienation in post-capitalist societal structures, but the fact that people weren't willing to accept their own beauty.

Most of her statements were met with bewilderment or scorn, but for some reason her belief that there was always more to take from life if you wanted it badly enough was met with a smattering of applause and a few horrified glances. An intermission was taken and the moderator pulled her off to the side and asked for her credentials. When she told her that she didn't have any credentials, the moderator had security escort her off the premises.

Elise always said that the path to positivity was fraught with difficulties and challenges, but she never thought it was actually going to be hard. She wandered around despondent for a few hours. She had so much to give—so much wisdom and positivity to share, but no one took her seriously. It was a horrible burden to have what everyone needed but no one was interested in.

Perhaps she was going about it wrong. Maybe starting with academic types wasn't where she was needed most. What she needed was to capture the voice of the youth—to strike a chord among her peers. The thought fascinated her and as she glanced at a community message board the answer came to her. On a flyer was an invitation to all musicians, poets and spoken word artists to an open mic session at the upcoming Greater Omaha Alternative Big Rawk Show! that was running the next day. She hurried back to her hotel suite and began to make preparations for the next day.

At about the same time Spook was shuffling into his limo, Elise was trying to assemble the perfect look for her venture into the wide world of edgy punk-dom. It was important to come across as "one of them" instead of someone who was, for example, concerned with hygiene. Elise carefully spent the next two hours applying make-up, teasing her hair and accessorizing. She finally had her look narrowed down to two choices: unbathed, but fresh-faced hippie and dead hooker. She chose the hippie look.

She stood in front of a mirror to practice her speech. She practiced how she'd show off her legs and draw attention to her chest. She practiced a winning smile and nodding with deep interest while taking a question. She practiced furrowing her brow as an imaginary audience member shared their personal story of heartbreak and spontaneously laughing at an amusing anecdote being told. As she checked her teeth for any stray piece of food, adjusted her newly purchased hemp jewelry and meticulously torn and threadbare t-shirt, Elise tried to focus her positivity on the challenge ahead. Elise vowed her positivity would be so radiant that those around her couldn't help but want to be just like her.

Vernon didn't want to be like Elise. He figured there was no way he'd be able to invest the amount of time in grooming alone, let alone the amount of bouncing and flittering she did was exhausting simply to watch. Vernon was vaguely contemplating Elise and a variety of other topics on a park bench. His motivation to visit the points of historical importance in Omaha had waned the previous day. He had ended up renting a cheap motel room and watching television until he fell asleep.

It had been nice to get back to old habits, he thought. Unfortunately, checkout was at eleven and the only thing

Vernon had to show for his night of semi-comfort was a much needed shower. Vernon counted through his pocket change. Of the $236.87 he had started with Vernon now had a bus ticket stub, two museum receipts, a paperclip and $15.32 mostly in one dollar bills and change. A man in a suit and shiny shoes sat down on the park bench with him. Vernon was too engrossed by the squabbling pigeons to take much notice.

"Is this seat taken?" asked the man.

Vernon looked at him and shook his head and then resumed his pigeon vigil.

"I'm sorry to have bothered you," said the man as he sat down next to Vernon. "I'm sorry, have we met before?"

Vernon looked at him again. He was a painfully average looking man that was also perfectly unknown to him. Vernon shrugged and answered "I don't think so."

"Well, is your name Vernon?"

Vernon looked back the man warily and nodded slowly. The man smiled widely and offered a handshake. He produced a badge out of his suit pocket and offered it at the same time as his hand.

"I've been looking for you for some time, Vernon," he said with a warm smile.

V

The police report was relatively uninteresting: the driver of Vehicle A swerved avoid hitting an animal as Vehicle B was making an unsignaled left hand turn. They struck each other in the intersection. Both vehicles were totaled in accident. The Driver of Vehicle B was arrested on outstanding warrants and the occupants of Vehicle A were arrested for a domestic disturbance stemming from an argument over the accident.

Like any incident there were a number of sides to it.

Rita was prowling public areas in her sporty red two-seater looking for ex-husband. There hadn't been any shooting sprees, hostage taking or naked screaming reported which, for Rita, was completely unacceptable. Vernon had to be revealed as the threat to normal decent society that would help Rita and Peter secure many happy lawsuits. She knew it would only be a matter of time, but the longer she went without news the more she feared that her seven figure settlement was in jeopardy.

She heard of the big music festival that was starting that day and desperately hoped that Vernon was there preparing to lace their espressos with arsenic. She was on her way when out of the corner of her eye she saw something that made her blood run cold. It looked like Vernon. And it looked like Vernon was being led—without incident—to a police cruiser. She wrenched her steering wheel to the left, hoping to intercept them in hopes of salvaging the scenario, or at least get her name mentioned prominently in a police report.

There was a sudden crackling groan and Rita was suddenly slapped in the face with a field of white. When she finally regained her bearings she found herself facing a different direction, her airbag deflating in her lap and a crowd forming around the scene. She stumbled out of the vehicle just in time to see Vernon waving good-bye to the police cruiser and then turn away with a start.

Rita began pointing and screaming incoherently at him, but he didn't react. Various on-lookers tried to restrain her and settle her down, but all she was able to do was scream in confused vengeance at the park bench where he was sitting oblivious to her presence. A large muscular police officer who had just arrived managed to subdue her and placed her in the backseat of his car.

When she had finally settled down, she realized that this could be an opportunity of its own and resolved to call Peter at the earliest opportunity to launch another civil action against the poor bastards who made the mistake of crossing paths with her. There was a rap at the window and Rita composed herself. The officer opened the door. "Are you Rita?" he asked.

"Yes officer. I'm sorry about earlier. I need to call my husband, he's a lawyer—"

"I know ma'am. You'll have plenty of opportunities to contact counsel at the station."

"At the station? No, no, you don't understand," she laughed at the officer's naiveté. "No, I just need the information so I can sue the pants of whoever hit me. I don't think criminal action will be necessary."

"I'm sorry ma'am, but you've got a warrant out. I'm placing you under arrest."

"There must be some mistake. I'm here to track down my sociopathic and dangerous ex-husband. I haven't done anything."

"Well, you can get more information on it when you're being processed in."

"Listen you stupid sonuvabitch, if you don't let me go right now I'm going to sue you until you'll have to take a loan out to refinance your fucking morning donuts. Is that what you want?!?"

"Watch you feet, ma'am."

And with that the officer closed the door. Rita began screaming again, but instead of invoking fear and menace it only caused a group of teenagers watching her to laugh and point.

Wayne just wanted a cold glass of orange juice. That's how it all started, somehow. Actually it had started with his imaginary tenure as a site manager for the Tulsa branch, but Wayne wasn't sure what happened with that just as he was pretty sure he didn't know how a cold glass of orange juice made him an asshole.

Yvonne for her part wasn't really explaining why he was an asshole as much as she was adding new transgressions and nasty names to his asshole status. With each passing mile Yvonne's rage grew. Soon Wayne was responsible for not only jeopardizing the financial situation, dooming their social situation, Yvonne's pregnancy and poor third world pollution regulation, but also the presence of evil itself in the universe.

Wayne would just nod and say "I'm sorry dear," or "I didn't mean to, dear," or "You're right dear." His meek willingness to accept her anger only fueled it further and suddenly Yvonne began slapping him. Wayne dared not raise his hand in defense, but just cringed and tried to keep an eye on the road. Yvonne let loose of flurry of flailing blows that temporarily blinded him. When he opened his eyes there was a large dog standing in the roadway, looking at him curiously. Wayne swerved when there was a flash of red squealing in front of him and then a sickening crunch and then an exploding pop.

As their SUV stopped moving, Wayne and Yvonne looked at each other in shock. Everything that had seemed so important was suddenly put in perspective for Wayne. They could have been hurt or even killed. The madman that swerved in front of them could be lying through his windshield dying for all Wayne knew. In that instant, Wayne came to grips with the vastness and beauty of life. He realized how every second was important and that it was imperative that the people you care about most knew how you felt about them. He was so moved that he turned to Yvonne to tell her how much he loved her. She was disheveled and lovely and so full of life. Wayne felt a lump rise in his throat as he gently rested his hand on her leg. Words weren't necessary. He could tell that she—

Yvonne punched Wayne in the nose.

"And that's for trying to kill me you codpiece!" she shrieked before she started hitting him with the rearview mirror that had been knocked loose by the impact. By the time the police arrived, Yvonne was kicking Wayne as he lay prostrate on the ground, moaning plaintively for mercy.

The police officers arrested Yvonne for domestic battery and Wayne for disorderly conduct when he refused to stop moaning and stand after Yvonne had been hauled away.

Vernon had been sitting on the park bench, looking at the badge. It was brassy and shiny and sparkled in the sunlight. Vernon wished he had one.

"That's nice," Vernon said.

The man looked at him curiously for a second and then just grinned again. "I've been trying to get a hold of you since the day they discharged you from the hospital, Vernon. You've given me quite a chase. I'm Wilbur Stein, special investigator with the FBI."

Vernon looked him over again. He seemed happy enough, although he was kind of a sweaty fellow with a slightly nervous quiver behind his voice.

"The doctor said I could go home," answered Vernon.

"Oh no, no, no Vernon," special investigator Wilbur Stein of the FBI chuckled. "You're not in trouble. I actually need a little help from you. It seems your ex-wife Rita and her lawyer friend have been doing a few things that aren't quite up to snuff. You see they took your house and sold it and then turned around and reinvested it in a number of illegal—well, I don't want to bore you with the details. The long and the short of it Rita and Peter are probably going to jail and you're in line to get your house back, and maybe a fair sight more if you've got a decent lawyer."

Vernon figured the money didn't much matter. The house was a convenience that he missed, however. He wanted to sit and watch television in his underwear again. He wanted to sit in his easy chair and not have to worry that a small child would be behind it, kicking it incessantly. He wanted to build the perfect plate rack.

Special investigator Wilbur Stein of the FBI had Vernon sign a couple of documents. Vernon vaguely remembered signing things for Peter and wondered if Peter could ever forgive his infidelity. Vernon figured that if he couldn't, then Peter would probably just die bitter and forlorn like spurned women in old novels.

Vernon heard a squeal of tires and crash. He looked up just in time to see his new friend from the FBI wave goodbye as he climbed into a waiting police cruiser. The officer in the car was playing chauffer for the big time special investigator from the coast and could have cared less about the automotive carnage playing out in his rear view mirror.

Vernon heard a familiar sound behind him and turned quickly. Purvis came trotting up and looked up at him expectantly. Vernon smiled and headed back to the park bench with his dog plodding up behind him. As Vernon kicked back on the park bench, Purvis flopped down next to him on the ground. Vernon wasn't worried about Doc, dogs like Doc always managed to find trouble but in the end nothing too bad could happen to a good dog.

The ghost was unhappy. After Wayne and Yvonne, after being hounded in the bus stop, after riding in the bus with Vernon and being duped by that devil woman, Margaux

Maddux, and after wandering around aimlessly in Omaha, the ghost was at the end of his rope. The world he had been fond of watching exist had turned into a horribly cruel, intolerable place that served no other purpose than to trample people when they were alive and irritate them when they were dead.

The ghost had made it most of the way through a park when he had given up. He sat down on a stump and gurgled melancholy blood bubbles as various animals and pets came by to harass him. The ghost was feeling particularly bad for himself as a small colony of squirrels decided to chatter at him and then defecate on his stump. The ghost began to wonder what possible end there could be to the indignities he was suffering.

Suddenly the squirrels became nervous and scampered up a nearby tree. The ghost saw a dog run by barking at them. It was the natural order of things—smaller annoying animals that would be chased off by larger ones who would in turn take their place in heckling the ghost. The ghost looked at the ground, hoping that his new tormentors would be short-lived. There was a prodding at his hand that was cool and furry.

The ghost blindly swatted at it until he realized that he had actually felt something. He looked up to see Doc, dead as a doornail with a big tire track across his midsection sitting happily wagging his tail at the ghost's feet. The ghost felt a burning energy in his bloated stomach. He didn't quite place the sensation.

The ghost looked up to see Purvis plodding across the street back to him and Doc when there was a screech of tires. An

SUV swerved violently narrowly missing Purvis and slammed into a little red sports car. Purvis surveyed the chaos and then ambled back towards the ghost.

The ghost recognized both cars. He limped towards the wreckage, Doc and Purvis in tow. When he saw Yvonne beating the hell out of Wayne and Rita being stuffed into a police cruiser the burning sensation became almost unbearable. The ghost realized the sensation—it was pure unadulterated elation.

As he gleefully watched Wayne simpering on the ground as his wife was handcuffed and Rita screaming obscenities helplessly from a passing police car, the ghost felt the warmth spread all around his body. Everything was white and glimmering as he happily stroked Doc behind his ears. The light grew brighter and brighter and suddenly Doc and the ghost were gone.

Purvis whimpered confused for a moment looking around for his companions. Then he noticed another familiar scent on the wind. He headed towards it and saw Vernon talking to a strange man. Purvis let out a little yawn and stretched against the cool grass before happily trotting over to his long lost owner.

All Things Right and Beautiful

I

Hey baby, it's me, the writer.

I think I should start seeing other readers.

Look, this book is going to end soon. This is probably the last real chapter and then I'm going to be leaving. We both knew that this couldn't last forever. I've got other projects to write and you've got a life outside of this book.

But we can still be friends. You can look me up for a nice casual reread sometime.

I mean it was great and all. I don't regret a thing, except maybe for the ending of "Time and Tide" but that had nothing to do with you. You should be happy for all the good times we had together. I mean, there was that time when Vernon made the sandwich and got tear-gassed. I really felt like we connected.

How about that thing with the plate rack? Pretty hot, right? All that innuendo and stuff—see, I'm old school—I believe the mind is the greatest erogenous zone. We had some pretty wild times, didn't we? But take heart, kiddo, you'll find someone else.

What do you mean you never liked "An Aside?" Look, there's no need to be all childish and defensive about—

What? Well, I faked my intros. Yeah, you heard me. I

haven't had a real intro since "Dinnertime" but didn't want to say anything that might hurt your feelings. If you weren't so needy maybe you'd realize that I wasn't getting what I needed out of this novel.

You know what, you can say all those things, but once my lawyer gets done with you you'll never get to see Vernon, the ghost, Spook, Doc, Purvis, Elise, Wayne, Yvonne, or Elise again. Not even for the holidays. Think about that when you're at home alone late at night.

Oh, I have intimacy issues?!? I don't see you reading "War and Peace" or "Atlas Shrugged". Think about it. You want intimacy, try something over three hundred pages. No answer for that, eh?

Listen, let's not fight in front of the characters, ok? Dr. Nash had a bad day at school today. He doesn't need to hear your little tantrum, alright?

This is for the best. You'll thank me someday.

II

The light faded gradually and shapes started to become more distinct. On a huge golden arch there was a sign that read "Welcome to *Heaven* ™: a nice place to spend eternity."

The ghost sighed. His body was still mangled and broken. Figures, he thought. Doc yawned and started trotting towards the gate. Next to the hulking golden doors was a little speaker that chirped serenely: "For your convenience you will be processed in the order you were received. Please take a number and wait for it to be called. And remember, here at *Heaven* ™, your satisfaction is our highest priority. Please enjoy your stay and feel free to leave any questions, comments or suggestions with your ascension assistance specialist. Thanks for choosing *Heaven* ™: a nice place to spend eternity."

Next to the speaker was a tag dispenser. The ghost took a tag and slid it into Doc's collar and then drew one for himself. The gates opened majestically to the sound of a heavenly choir singing "The Girl From Iponema." The ghost and Doc walked through and found themselves standing in a vast waiting room. Overhead was a huge marquee that said "Now Serving" with a number below it. The number would change every couple seconds with a little signal bell as the number flopped over. At the moment it read 4,368. The ghost's number was 3,472,601. Doc's number was 3,472,600.

There were a number of little makeshift groups throughout the waiting area all quietly chatting with each other. The ghost didn't recognize anyone and was about to sit over by himself when he felt a hand on his shoulder. He turned and let out a gurgled scream. Someone had made a terrible mistake—the ghost was in hell.

"You've heard the song on the radio. It's one of the true grunge classics of our day and now we are pleased to introduce, appearing for the first time on our stage—The Chalupa Ponies!"

There was a smattering of largely apathetic applause as Spook, acoustic guitar in hand made his way to the mic at center stage. There they were; a thousand eyes trained on him waiting to be amused and entertained. Spook sighed.

He could've been getting a complimentary massage courtesy of Chetsoft right now and he wouldn't have to amuse anyone.

"This song is called 'Political Maniacal.' I hope you like it."

And with that Spook took his first tentative steps into stardom. And by "tentative" I mean "not very good." The mic started to feedback and suddenly Spook forgot where he was in the song. He kept playing in hopes no one would notice and thought he had succeeded until he realized that he was playing the theme from "Shaft." He abruptly stopped and pretended like that was what he had meant to do.

He tried to build some momentum by launching into "Elise is a Dumb Bitch Who Doesn't Care About Anyone But Herself (Periwinkle Death)." Unfortunately the full force of his poor beaten acoustic guitar wasn't enough to convince the masses below to start a mosh pit. He was just getting to the bridge when a string broke and again he was left trying to regain his bearings. As he stumbled through the solo and the chorus one more time he saw groups of people getting up to stand in line for the portable toilets or browsing through the various festival vendors' wares.

He mumbled "I'll be back in a second" and made his way to the side of the stage to restring his guitar, trying to desperately find a way to prove to the crowd that the Chalupa Ponies were the next big thing. Was the next best thing. Dammit.

"Hey kid," came a voice from backstage. Spook looked up

to see an old man chomping on a cigar standing in the wings. "You're the kid from the hold music, right?"

Spook nodded.

"Look kid, this isn't brain surgery. They came to hear one song—the one they play on the radio. Don't try to win 'em over with a bunch of shit they never heard before, okay? Play the song they paid money to hear and then do whatever the hell you want. Take a shit on stage for all I care, but at least then you know they'll be paying attention. And don't get so nervous. Makes you look like a big pussy."

Spook didn't know exactly how to react to either the idea of defecating in front of a festival crowd or being called a pussy. He just nodded and headed back to the stage. He let out another sigh and said "This is song is called 'Sweet Piece Elise...'"

Elise had heard her name over the PA system as she walked away from the tent where she had been ousted a few moments before and had turned to see who had said it. She was hoping for a glimmer of goodness to redeem her experience thus far.

At the open mic event she had registered and subsequently learned that it was a bit of a competition. Each presenter was paired with another and given a time limit. Then, after it both had finished the winner would be determined by the audience applause.

The first round she had been paired against a middle aged unemployed former telemarketer named James L. Curtis.

He was wearing a tattered suit and obviously hadn't bathed in weeks. He wreaked of alcohol and urine.

Elise bravely took the stage and smiled brightly to everyone in the audience. She took out her notecards, cleared her throat and began.

"Hi, my name is Elise and I've come to talk to you about something that I find very troubling. In a world where there is so much beauty and things to be happy about, so many of us are caught up in a whirlwind of self-doubt, negativity and other bad things. Many people begin to lose hope and wonder if life really does have any happiness for them. I'm here to assure each and every one of you that there is.

"Now I know what some of you are thinking. 'Elise, you seem to have it together, but look at me—I'm not as attractive or outgoing as you. How can you tell me that there's happiness out there for me?' Well, I can say it because the Elise you see before you is only pretty and outgoing because I believe that there is happiness out there for me. Of course you might not all be as objectively pretty as me, but that's no reason to believe that life is any less good and beautiful. The thing to remember all the time is that positivity is your key to true happiness.

"I'm sure a lot of you have questions and I'd be happy to take a few. This is just a brief introduction and I think we could all learn best from each other instead of just listening to me."

Elise smiled widely and looked expectantly at the crowd. There was utter silence throughout the tent. Elise kept smiling and waiting for a question.

She saw some motion towards the back of the tent and pointed and said "Yes, you in the back there," as supportively and encouragingly as she could.

The young man stood nervously as everyone turned to look at him. He pointed at himself as if unsure whether he was being addressed. Elise smiled and nodded and tried to show off her legs a little bit.

"Um," he replied.

"Go ahead, it's okay. We're all friends here."

"Uh—"

"Could I have you speak up a bit? It's hard to hear you up here," Elise flashed another grin. Success was at hand.

"Well—"

"Oh, and could you tell me your name?"

"Uh, Jason."

"Okay Jason, what would you like to share with us?"

"Um, nothing, really..."

"Now Jason, you've shown a lot of courage just to stand up today. It would be a shame for you to quit after doing the hardest part. Feel free to tell me whatever is on your mind."

"I dunno..."

The audience was entranced at the exchange between one of their own and Elise. Elise could feel it. Every eye was focused on him and every ear on her voice. This would be her defining moment.

"Go ahead Jason. I doubt you can say anything that we all haven't felt before."

Victory was at hand. Elise was daydreaming about the little inspirational messages she would write on the inside covers during her book signings. "Always stay positive, Love Elise" or "Just because you have stomach cancer don't forget that life is beautiful. Keep fighting! Elise." It would be grand.

"Well, I was thinking that even though you're kinda hot, this is lame, and that the chick running the tie-dye stand was cute and I could probably stand to talk to her for a while. Oh, and I have to take a dump, too." The audience chuckled as Jason excused himself from the tent.

Elise was feeling faint. She felt her face flush red and her voice cracked as she asked the audience again, "Does anyone have any questions?"

She let out a sigh of relief as a single hand in the back was tentatively raised. "Yes, go ahead."

A tall pale skinny girl with jet-black dyed hair and glasses stood up. Elise thought she could be a lot prettier with some makeup and more flattering wardrobe choices.

"Uh, yeah. I don't get it. Is this supposed to be funny or ironic or something?" she asked matter-of-factly.

"What?"

"And time's up. Everyone give a hand to Elise for her, um, little speech thing," interrupted the emcee.

There were a couple token claps and a catcall.

Elise would have been cut, but James L. Curtis proceeded to stumble onto the stage, cursing the audience and all other little shitheads who would conspire to have a hardworking decent, honest man like him fired for something he didn't do. What was more, all those cocksuckers could go to hell for ruining his life and he wouldn't give two pisses for it. He then proceeded to vomit over the side of the stage and fall face down wailing that Jesus didn't love him anymore until he passed out.

No one clapped for James L. Curtis making Elise the winner by default.

Elise put on a brave face for the next round but was soundly ousted by a lesbian poet who talked about orgasms, "the Man," and the difficulty of finding true love in a heterosexual world. As she made her way out of the tent not one person stopped to encourage her or to confide that they had felt the way she had described. More of them were actually talking about James L. Curtis who had been forcibly removed by event security as he screamed that he would exact his revenge on them all.

She shuffled out defeated when she heard someone say her name over the PA, or so she thought. Suddenly familiar chords started to ring out and the crowd, which had been mulling about indifferently began to reverberate with excitement. Elise squinted towards the stage and saw Spock or Speck or whatever he had called himself. He was singing the song he had played for her the day they had sex and everyone seemed to love it.

An idea reverberated across Elise's brain: she would make him hers and then use his position to spread her message to the thronging masses. "When circumstances in your life seem to make everything difficult, just remember: circumstances are just the fertilizer that beautiful flowers need to grow!" Elise smiled as she made her way towards the stage. She was getting ready to blossom in all her glory and she had found the means to her happiness. It was just a matter of being willing to take it.

III

"It's right there, just waiting for you take it," wheezed the man. Within minutes of special investigator Wilbur Stein of the FBI's departure the man had pulled up in his luxury import sedan and waddled up to Vernon. He handed Vernon a business card that Vernon had pretended to read. The man was out of breath, but tried to get himself together before launching into his presentation.

"I've been looking for you for some time, Vernon. When I heard about the horrible injustice perpetrated upon you I was stirred to action. When I heard how everything was stripped from you—your home, your possessions, your dignity—by a couple of amoral opportunists willing to sink to any depths in order to line their pockets with the blood, sweat and tears of an honest, hard-working man like yourself, well, it sickened me, sir. I was physically sickened, my hand to God. And when I had finished being sick I was sick again, just because of how morally repugnant the whole story was to me.

"And then I thought to myself, what can be done to punish those who would take advantage of those who have fallen on hard times? What can be done to prevent something this egregious from ever happen again? And then I realized that I was uniquely qualified to assist you and those like you in making sure justice is done."

"Um," said Vernon.

"No, no, please, it's my pleasure to offer you this service. It comes with no cost to you unless we win, and then I'll just take a percentage of the judgment as a token of gratitude for the long hours and hard work that the most aggressive legal services available would warrant. Now has the FBI been in contact with you?"

Vernon nodded.

"That's wonderful. You see, the FBI can help us a lot with this. With the seizure and criminal charges, we now have a leg up on them. They can say that you're mentally unstable and cannot be trusted because of that little run-in you had with the S.W.A.T. team a couple months ago, but we can stand up and point to the federal indictment and they can't deny that or try to explain it away as groundless. But before that thought alone makes you comfortable, know that they will lash back at you with all they have. And inevitably the rule of law will waiver, leaving them with little more than a slap on the wrist and you will be given next to nothing as reparation for the suffering you've endured at their hands.

"Don't you see, the law may be satisfied with probation time—allowing them to run free, while you have to struggle to reclaim the life you had. But I am here to make sure that justice is done, even if that means going above and beyond what the criminal courts have the power and desire to enforce. I will get you your life back, Vernon, and I will bleed them until your pain is justly compensated."

Vernon sat back in the bench watching the fat little man wheeze and gesture frantically. It reminded him of a man who tried to convince him to buy a used Plymouth years before. Purvis was lying on his side, only half watching the lawyer. Purvis didn't know about just compensation or the rule of law, he just wanted something to chew on. Or something rancid to smell. Either way.

The ghost was still rancid. The ghost's face was still in a horrible grimace of fear and loathing as the last bloody gurgles escaped his mouth.

"Goodness, looks like someone needs to relax a little bit," chuckled Margaux Maddux. "Well, I was just coming by to see if you needed anything. My name's Margaux and I'm your afterlife acclamation liaison. Are you here with anyone?"

The ghost let out a terrified squeak.

"No one? Well that just won't do. It's important to begin

socializing with others as soon as possible. After all, it may be **Heaven** ™ but that doesn't mean you can just sit and wait for happiness to come to you. You have to be willing take it and you're not going to be taking anything with attitude, Mr. Shy Pants," Margaux smiled with syrupy patronization.

"Um, he's with us," came a timid offering. The ghost looked and saw a short thin man with a huge gash in his head. "He just kinda wandered off is all. It's alright Ms. Maddux, we'll watch out for him, you don't need to worry about it."

Margaux looked at him skeptically. "Mr. McGwire, you're not fibbing me, are you? You know as well as anyone that the orientation is very important to help nurture and develop the kind of positive thinking that **Heaven** ™ is all about."

"Of course, Ms. Maddux, I'd never lie to you. We were honestly just looking for him."

"Well, I suppose if he's with you I don't have to worry about finding him an Eternity Buddy," she turned her attention back to the ghost. "Oh, and who's this with you?" she asked as she knelt down to Doc.

"Who's a good dog? Are you going to be a good puppy while you're here? Of course you are. Of course you are," she said in a baby-talk voice.

She abruptly stood up, her demeanor at once was stern. "The dog has to go, Mr. McGwire, you know that. I won't have my waiting area trodden on by animals of any sort, let alone some mutt. You understand? Take that thing to *Doggy Heaven* ™ immediately."

The other ghost nodded submissively. "Of course, Ms. Maddux, whatever you say. It'll be done right away."

Margaux's expression changed back to her unnervingly cheery smile that she had first exhibited. "Well, that's all I wanted to hear, Mr. McGwire. You and your friend can go on together. You'll be processed in the order you arrived. And thanks for choosing *Heaven* ™."

And with that she turned and started interfering with some other new arrivals who didn't look positive enough.

When she was out of earshot, the other ghost gestured frantically for the ghost to follow him. "Hey, my name's Mac. You got to steer clear of that one. She can make life difficult for you if she wants to, and from the looks of you, she'll probably want to."

Mac led the ghost to a little cluster of the waiting dead. They each had rather distinct injuries, decapitations and the like. "We're not allowed to be up front," whispered Mac. "The powers that be want everyone to think *Heaven* ™ is a place where everything is right and beautiful with little cherub babies and angels floating around. When someone like Joe here comes in after falling into a vat of industrial waste, they need to find a place to put them out of sight."

The charred, black skeletal figure gave a half wave to the ghost, "Hey, how's it goin'?"

The ghost nodded in reply.

"The worst part of all this is that she'll come and take your number. I've been here since 1911—lost my number four times," sighed Mac. "She'll come swooping in and say that you've been referred to a different associate and you've been issued a new ascension number. Then she'll take it and head over to some person just came in after suffering a stroke or some other thing that lets them look normal and give them your number. I almost made it the other day, but wouldn't you know it, some pretty young thing who died while getting breast implants came in. so I lost it."

"That's nothing," muttered a woman who was holding her decapitated head. "I lost my number to a swimsuit model who OD'd. I mean, is she even supposed to be here? It makes no sense."

The ghost looked over his new-found compatriots deep in thought. Doc flopped down at his feet.

"Good Christ, if she sees that, it'll be all our asses," muttered Joe.

"No shit. Mac, you gotta tell him to get rid of it," piped up a ghost in the back covered with oozing sores. "Some of us would like to at least have a chance of getting our new bodies sometime before Armageddon."

There was a collective sigh of frustration that came from the group. "I can only imagine what would happen if we're still around then," grumbled the headless lady.

"You think they're backlogged now? Geez, we wouldn't

see a number under a billion for eons. If we don't get in before it happens we might as well forget about it afterwards. They love those war heroes almost as much as they love babies."

As soon as the word "babies" was uttered another groan went up from the group. The ghost just watched them all as he scratched Doc behind his ears. He had spent thirty odd years being dead and for the first time he felt that there was something he was supposed to do.

Spook had almost lost his place when the audience had erupted. He looked for the easiest exit in case they had finally decided to riot, but instead the audience looked as if they had always been enjoying themselves. Spook looked offstage and saw the old man puffing away on his cigar nodding as if to say "I told you so." After seeing what an apathetic crowd was like, Spook decided to go with the moment and enjoy it. He was playing extended bridges, making up words, stage diving and for five minutes Spook was the epicenter of cool.

As he finally hit the final turnaround Spook looked down at the crowd and saw Elise standing there, beaming. This was SO the Chalupa Ponies mystique he thought to himself as he let the adulation of the audience wash over him. He was so going to get some, he thought.

The rest of the set was much like it had began. The onlookers mulled around, although a few actually hung out and listened intently. Spook finished the last song to a warm smattering of applause and walked off the stage.

"Not bad kid. Like I said, they only really wanted to hear

one song, but you did good," the old man said as he gently chewed the end of his cigar. "Listen, I handle a number of artists. I think you have some potential. Of course, you'll have to work your skinny ass off. That 'Sweet Piece' song will only get you so far. You're gonna have to spend a lot of time playing clubs and opening for bands that don't give a shit about you, but I think you might be able to make some noise if you keep at it."

The old man reached into his suit pocket and flipped out a card. "If you think you're ready to take a crack at it, gimme a call. I gotta run. Take 'er easy."

Spook looked at the card. He was excited, but the talk of working hard definitely didn't sound like part of the Chalupa Ponies mystique. And not being instantaneously adored was definitely not what the Chalupa Ponies were about. If his revenge on those little turncoat fucks in Jimmy Hoffa's Missing Head wasn't immediate, it really didn't feel nearly as satisfying.

He felt an arm wrap around his waist. He spun around, startled to find Elise smiling, showing off her cleavage and legs as she gave him a little squeeze.

"Oh Speck, that was so wonderful," she bubbled.

IV

Vernon wasn't fond of the lawyer, but he had a car and had plenty of things to say while he drove Vernon back to his newly reclaimed home. The lawyer was as interested in Vernon's pain and suffering as Dr. Nash had been in Vernon's plate rack.

"You see Vernon, the fact that she drove you to a nervous breakdown and then took your house is the kind of thing juries eat up," the lawyer panted. "The jury will see her and that shyster husband of hers for exactly what they are —a couple wolves in sheep's clothing just using you for their own personal gain. You're lucky I tracked you down, Vernon. There are a lot of attorneys out there who would just try to use this as a big pay day instead of seeing it as a moral imperative to do what's right—"

"—For a small percentage," replied Vernon.

"Exactly!" beamed the lawyer. "No hourly rate, no huge staff, and only a few additional expenses that aren't covered. When this all began I looked in the mirror and said to myself: 'This is the kind of thing that could keep you from getting the swimming pool, but dadgummit, it's the right thing to do, so pool be damned!'"

Purvis lay on his side in the backseat, tongue flopping around like a dancing marionette as Vernon reached back and scratched his stomach. Purvis didn't much care about suffering or punishment, he was just happy that he was on his way home and that he was forever safe from Carson and Renee. Vernon looked back at him and Purvis gave a satisfied warble in response.

Vernon wasn't sure what to make of the lawyer's offer. He felt inclined to go along with him just because he had given him a ride home. It could be one of those turning points where everything could be grand and easy. It wasn't that he couldn't use the money. Using money is never difficult; it's keeping money from using you that seemed to get people all hung up.

Elise was all hung up on the Spook. Her arms were around his shoulders as he made his way through the crowd. A few asked for autographs or asked him questions about the Chalupa Ponies. Spook made sure to show off the fine piece of ass on his arm the whole time. But the old man's words haunted him. He wasn't sure why he should want to work hard to be a big rock star. He had the money, courtesy of Chetsoft and his executive vice-president position, and now he had a hot girlfriend. He wasn't sure if he really wanted to try and work his way up the ladder.

"So, Speck, what have you been up to? I haven't seen you since, well, since that day," Elise started getting teary eyed and watched for Spook's reaction.

"Don't worry about it, baby. Spook's here. You wanna go backstage and fool around?"

"Oh, Speck, I feel so safe in your arms. Are you going to be a big rock star and take care of me?"

"I dunno, babe. You can't fence me in. Besides, I got the sweet gig as this executive VP of Internal Affairs and Efficiency. It's pretty sweet."

Elise smiled to herself as she clung to Leonard. "That sounds so important—so much cooler than just some rock singer. I bet you have all sorts of people at your beck and call. That's so sexy."

Leonard just paused for a moment and thought about his options. "Yeah, I just did the music thing as a joke, anyway. The tech market is where it's at. You think that's hot, baby?"

"You know I do," smiled Elise as she started figuring out how much she could do on an executive VP's salary.

"What's all this muttering about" came a voice behind them. The others cowered in fear, many trying to hide behind Mac. The ghost turned slowly, to face her.

"Um, nothing Ms. Maddux. We were just talking about how good it will be once we finally get our new bodies, is all," offered Mac timidly.

"Yes, it will. *Heaven* ™ is especially generous to the downtrodden as you all well know. Speaking of which, where's Joseph?"

The blackened skeleton cringed at the mention of his name and slowly rose.

"Ah, Joseph, we have especially downtrodden aerobics instructor who has just arrived. There have been a few changes made and you've been assigned to another associate."

If Joe had lips, the bottom one would have been surely quivering. "But, Ms. Maddux, I'm scheduled to go in the next couple hours. Perhaps there's been a mistake?"

"Now Joseph," Margaux growled sternly, "I know I don't have to tell you how things work around here. I wouldn't have reassigned you if it wasn't very important, would I?"

Joe dropped his head and muttered, "No, Ms. Maddux."

"That's it, Joseph. I'm sure you'll go through soon with your new associate, anyway. Now I must be—"

Margaux stopped mid-sentence as Doc ambled up to her and started sniffing her crotch.

"Oh shit," whispered Mac to himself.

"Mr. McGwire, what the living hell is this... animal still doing here? I gave you specific instructions that this mutt was to be taken immediately to **Doggy Heaven** ™. Why is it still here?"

"Oh, well, we, um, lost track of time?"

Margaux snatched Doc's collar and stuck her finger just below Mac's nose, "I've put up with your little bullshit games long enough, Mr. McGwire. Perhaps it's time I took a look at all your assignments. I'll be back after I take care of this mangy creature and you better have your numbers ready!"

Margaux turned trying to drag Doc away and walked right into the ghost.

"Don't think that because you're new here that you're going to get any special treatment," she tried to walk around him, but the ghost stepped sideways to stay in front of her. Margaux's expression was one of confused rage.

"What the hell do you think you're doing? Are you retarded?" she growled.

The ghost leaned into her face, his broken and purple face inches from hers. His blackened eyes stared unblinking into hers. Margaux recoiled from his hideous form, but the ghost kept leaning towards her. Margaux turned her head away, refusing to look him in the eyes. The ghost narrowed his swollen eyes and let out a menacing hiss that made little bubbles of blood and rot seethe behind his crushed teeth.

"Mr. McGwire, tell your associate that he's playing with fire. This behavior is—"

The ghost lurched forward right in front of Margaux's face. He let his shattered jaw drop and began flailing his tongue at her while making sickly coughing noises. Margaux tried to push him away, but the ghost grabbed her hand and began drooling on her arm.

"Mr. McGwire! Mr. McGwire!" cried Margaux in alarm, but the ghost wouldn't let go. She released Doc's collar and tried to push the ghost away.

The waiting dead stood watching in awe. The fearsome, unshakable and formidable Margaux Maddux was now whimpering like an offended child at the presence of the ghost's mangled form. Her repulsion left her paralyzed. She was helpless to combat the ghost's horrible unblinkingly immediate ugliness. Even with all her positivity and iron fisted grasp on claimed happiness, she could do nothing against the very real horror in front of her.

"Mr. McGwire, please! You can keep the dog, just get him away from me!" wailed Margaux.

The ghost shook his head from side to side violently letting drool, blood and broken teeth spray everywhere. He let out a guttural groan of irritation at her. It had been her that had tortured him on the bus. It had been because of her boot-licking little follower Elise that he had been forced to endure Wayne and Yvonne. All his helplessness and frustration had finally found their receptacle. She had tortured him—even from beyond the grave, but now when brought face to face with him he would have his revenge.

"Um, I think he's saying that he keeps the dog and we don't have to change our numbers ever again," offered Mac.

"Don't you start with me. You've all had it when this is over!" cried Margaux defiantly.

She pulled away from the ghost and fled down to the block of cubicles where the other liaisons and mid-level office staff.

Mac and the others looked at each other in disbelief. Either something very good or very bad had just happened. Doc for his part was satisfied to lick himself and ignore the hubbub. "Dude, we're so screwed," whispered Joe. "We'll be lucky if they just assign us to clean purgatory for the rest of eternity."

"Maybe if we scattered they won't be able to find us," offered the headless lady.

The ghost wasn't listening to them. They didn't know who they were up against. They feared Margaux Maddux and those like her. The ghost wasn't afraid of anything anymore. He had lived with Rita. He had survived Wayne and Yvonne. He had lost Doc and Purvis and his home—not to mention he had been brutally murdered. Whatever this place had, he knew it wouldn't have the rocks to stop him.

A small group of office staff, following Margaux's frantic pointing and whispering slowly moved towards the ghost. The waiting dead tried to look like they didn't know the ghost or were doing something else, but out of the corner of their eyes they watched everything intently.

What the others didn't see was the fear in the eyes of Margaux and her fellow staff. They approached in a mass huddle, each appeared ready to scream and run at the slightest provocation. An unwilling volunteer was pushed to the front of the group as they approached. He was a tall man with sandy hair and boyish features. His *Heaven* ™ nametag read Todd.

"Um, I understand that we're having some difficulties here," he said in a quivering voice.

The ghost stood motionless, staring at him in a silent challenge. Todd looked back his co-workers and the prodded him on.

"Well, Margaux here says that you were very rude to her and that you refused to turn over your ascension number. While I realize that you're not technically required to do so, failure to follow a staff request can significantly delay your processing not to mention create difficulties for others awaiting processing."

Todd looked at the ghost expectantly, hoping desperately that his explanation had convinced the ghost to be a good little dead person and go with the flow. The ghost looked at Todd somberly and then reached up and peeled off a tattered piece of scalp from his own head. Todd grimaced as the ghost held it up for all to see. The ghost looked at Todd again and then flicked the bloody bit of hair and skin in Todd's face.

"Oh God, that's just... I mean, oh, the smell—there's no reason for that. You're not impressing anyone, you know. I got some in my mouth—sweet Jesus it's horrible," sputtered Todd.

The ghost stood watching Todd do a little dance of disgust trying to get the ghost's rotting flesh off of his body. The ghost began laughing at him with a horrible wet wheezing gurgling laugh. Todd looked at the ghost helplessly, realizing that his words had no affect. Todd turned to his co-workers for help, sympathy and assistance. What he saw was the better part of the office pool looking queasy and the others were turning pale with shock and terror.

Margaux Maddux suddenly strode up to the ghost angrily. "You are an ugly, negative, irresponsible and insensitive excuse of a man. No one cares about something as broken and ugly as you. You're here because we say you can be here. *Heaven* ™ is about us—about the people who care enough to be beautiful and give of themselves. You—you're just... just a disgusting petty little man who doesn't know your place."

The ghost stood staring at Margaux. The office pool and the waiting dead stood staring to see what would happen next. There was silence. Was the ghost deflated? Had Margaux's words humiliated him back to submission? Would the natural order be restored?

The ghost dropped his head. The office staff held their breath, hoping that this insane revolution had ended. The waiting dead hoped that the ghost could find his second wind and deliver them from the tyranny of their mid-level tormentors. And then, it happened.

For the first time since 1964, the ghost spoke. It was a dull rumbling from his chest. At first no one had even realized he had said anything, but the ghost repeated it. The color drained from Margaux's face. The others retreated back to their cubicles. The ghost looked at them with his black eyeballs, shattered leg, bloody and broken skull and any number of other debilitating injuries and grunted "And what are you going to do about it?"

Todd backed away slowly, his face ashen with shame and fear. The ghost had broken Margaux Maddux. That was for that goddamned magazine quiz, he thought to himself.

V

Vernon walked into his house for the first time in months. The place had been repainted with off-whites and earth tones and there was the faint smell of cat piss in the air.

"I wasn't able to get most of your stuff back, I'm afraid," the lawyer wheezed as he followed Vernon and Purvis inside. "We can add that to our damages, though. The only things that were still in storage are over there."

Covered in a sheet were Vernon's old beaten easy chair, his

old portable television and an odd assortment of plate racks. Vernon moved the easy chair back to its old location and set up the TV in front of it. Purvis took his place on the floor next to recliner and Vernon turned on the television and tried to adjust the tuning.

"Um, you'll have plenty of time for that in a bit, Vernon. We should probably discuss how we're going to proceed with our case," suggested the lawyer.

Vernon sat down in the recliner and absent-mindedly reached down to scratch Purvis behind the ears. "What if I don't want there to be a case?" he asked nonchalantly.

"Now I know it might seem scary at first, Vernon, but rest assured, you'll have the most vigorous representation money can buy in me. I'm not going to lie to you and say it's all going to be fruit and roses, but the little discomfort you'll have to suffer through the legal process will be amply rewarded in punitive damages.

"Besides, what are you going to do for money, Vernon? I didn't want to bring this up, but you'll never get your job back at the insurance company and you really don't have any prospects. What little you have that hasn't been frozen by the FBI pending the prosecution of Rita and Peter could last you a few months, at most. This lawsuit can get you back into the black and give you enough money to live out the rest of your natural life without having to worry about working ever again."

"I don't worry about working ever again," replied Vernon.

"You're missing my point, Vernon, this can help you gain

the freedom to pursue your dreams. This could be you opportunity to get ahead in life."

Vernon shrugged. He had come to terms that his dreams would always be sweeter unattained then if he chased them. Dreams always seemed kinda like the prom queen to Vernon. Everyone wanted her, but only a handful were still happy to have her after being in the backseat with her. And those were the ones that were usually dumped by the prom queen the next day. It was a cycle.

As for opportunity, Vernon didn't see a need for it. He'd been on a vacation and seen scenic Omaha. He'd gotten his house back and one of his dogs and had the closest thing to an adventure that he ever really ever cared to have. Opportunity was the same as drama and quite frankly, Vernon had enough of drama to last him the rest of his life. It was all far too busy for him—all the chasing and the wanting and the lusting. And when it all came down usually all you had was a mess and maybe alimony. It was so much more relaxing to just let it all come and go and just enjoy the show.

Vernon sighed. The fat wheezy little man's face was turning red. "I'll call you if I decide to do it," Vernon offered.

"Well, I'm in the office the rest of the week" the lawyer chattered excitedly. "You just let the secretary know who you are and I'll take your call anytime, day or night. I'm the man for the job, Vernon, just you wait and see."

The little man waved and waddled happily out of the house. Vernon adjusted the reception and wondered if the lawyer realized he didn't have a phone. Purvis let out a little whimper as Vernon stopped petting him.

Vernon smiled at Purvis and consoled him with "It's alright. I was just going to see if there was something around we could get you to eat."

Epilogue:

A Warning from the Future (Clean Your Plate)

I

I am future writer!

You can tell I'm far superior by the font I'm using—from the future. Your pithy primitive intellect cannot begin to fathom what I am about to share with you. I can see that you are trying to understand what I represent. Save your energy, for I come from a point in the future and my writing powers have exceeded anything you can comprehend.

Yes, believe it or don't, but I speak to you from the year... 2010! Yes, our technology is light years ahead of yours. Your greatest accomplishments are little more than quaint children's trinkets in the year 2010. Bow and be amazed, for I am the bearer of the future wisdom! Do not shield your eyes from the inescapable tale of Vernon—from the year 2010!

It may be the only thing that can save your worthless race.

II

Elise strapped on her jet pack as she screamed "I'm the best thing that ever happened to you, you sorry piece of shit! You'll be sitting here all alone and then you'll realize how much you love me and then it will be too late!"

Leonard stood looking at ground, nodding without really meaning it. He just murmured "Yes dear," over and over mechanically. He had been doing that a lot since he had been fired as the executive vice president of Internal Affairs and Efficiency. Leonard began to wonder if it had been a good idea to "accidentally" drop Elise's Margaux Maddux paraphernalia into the molecular transducer instead of the "Mr. Handi-Pack" robotic mover. Leonard had to fight off a grin and had to fake a cough while he tried to regain his somber expression.

"You little faggot, I see you trying to laugh," Elise hissed. "You know, the only reason I stayed with you as long as I did was because of that goddamn apocalypse. You were such a horrible lay that I almost left while the bombs were falling and the war robots were marching leveling everything in sight! I would have been better off if I'd married Corey Fucking Burton! I hope you die!"

And with that, Elise was gone. Leonard sighed and sat down on the sofa. The videophone rang. Leonard grumbled as he had to go answer it. The screen flickered to life and a horribly wrinkled toothless man was there, grinning at him.

"Is this Leonard?"

Leonard nodded.

"Ha ha! I've visited my threefold vengeance on you, after all these years! Now it is time to reveal that you've been suffering at the wrathful hands of James L. Curtis! Ha ha ha ha!"

"Um, who?"

The old man stopped laughing and looked irritated. "James L. Curtis, that's me. I'm the one who has been punishing you!"

"Do I know you?"

"You had better. You stole my life from me, stripped me of my dignity, my employment and drove me to the bottle."

"Um." replied Leonard.

"Oh for Chrissakes, I was on the Monolith Bank Account. You got me fired for doing nothing and plunged me into a dark vortex of self-loathing and destructive behavior..."

"Um, ok, I think I kinda..."

"You don't remember me at all, do you?"

Leonard shrugged. "Sorry if things didn't work out for you," he offered.

"Oh but they have! My three fold vengeance is a brilliant success!" cackled James L. Curtis.

"Three fold?"

"First I had you fired from your job! And then I managed to drive a wedge between you and your lovely wife! Ha ha ha ha ha!"

Leonard shrugged. He really hadn't been that interested in his job anyway, as for Elise, her leaving was probably one of the nicer things James L. Curtis could have done for him. Leonard stopped for a moment, wasn't there supposed to be three things?

"What was the third thing?" Leonard asked.

"What?"

"The third thing. You said your vengeance was three fold, doesn't that mean there should be a third thing?"

"Um, well, you had just gotten comfortable in your chair and you had to leave to answer the phone. Ha ha!"

Leonard sighed, "Well, it was great talking to you again. Nice work on that vengeance thing, you really got me. We'll have to do it again sometime."

"Sure thing, buddy. Hey no hard feelings, alright?"

"No worries. Have a good one."

"You too."

Click.

Leonard sighed as another mechanical war robot trampled above the bunker as it breathed fire. The war was over everywhere except in Omaha, apparently. He vaguely wondered if living under martial law wasn't some kind of metaphor for being married.

III

Slowly the waiting dead were processed through. First it was Joe who did a stiff-legged little crumbly dance on his way down the row of cubicles. Then it was oozing guy and headless lady who had their number called. Then it was Mac.

Mac headed up to the ghost with a wide smile.

"Well, I've been here since 1911 and now I'm finally having my day. I have to think that you're the reason I didn't have to wait even longer for this. I hear rumors that the Apocalypse is coming. You think you'll be alright?"

The ghost gurgled an affirmative with a shrug. Didn't much matter to him, really.

"Well, I'll watch for you. They say *Heaven* ™ is plenty big, but you can always find who you're looking for. We'll have to have coffee when you get there, okay?"

Mac shook the ghost's shattered limp hand and then departed with a half-wave down the aisle. That had been a while ago. The ghost didn't mind though, Doc was still around and the quiet activity was strangely soothing.

The Apocalypse had come and gone, but Margaux Maddux never came back to try to make someone change their number. The ghost had taken a seat in the main waiting area but no one had told him to leave. He had sat there with Doc for a long time, just happy to sit and watch people come and go. It was a lot like the old days on the porch.

The casualties of the great final battle were beginning to pile up behind him, but the ghost wasn't that interested. There was a time and place for everything. His basement in 1964 was apparently the time and place to have the living hell beat out of you with a hammer. Whatever year it was now apparently was the time for giant robotic war machines to tromp across the globe shooting death rays from their eyes with nuclear missiles dropping from the sky like raindrops.

The heavenly choir music had begun doing big band standards a while ago and was just starting to transition to Vegas classic standards with "You're Nobody Til Somebody Loves You." If this was eternity, it probably wouldn't be too bad. Doc scratched behind his ears as the overhead sign dinged 3,472,597.

Ding. 3,472,598

Ding. 3,472,599...

IV

Vernon was washing his hands. Vernon had remembered when liquid hand soap was a big deal. Now it was all about being translucent anti-bacterial hyper-hygienic happy good time liquid hand soap. The side of the bottle proudly proclaimed that it killed 99.9% of all microscopic whoozits. Vernon wondered that if the .1% of the little buggers were just lucky or particularly resilient. He wasn't sure which was worse, the bacteria that had an uncanny knack for avoiding certain sanitary soapy doom or the ones that were resistant to the soap's toxic powers.

Vernon sighed. He was older now with thinning gray hair, a slight hunch and eyeglasses. RoboPurvis, his cyborg dog, sat by the worn easy chair recharging his batteries. Vernon walked into the kitchen and began making a cheese sandwich and a bowl of chicken soup.

Vernon took his soup and sandwich into the basement. There, lining the walls, neatly stacked were hundreds of plate racks. Some were large and ornate, some were small and simple. Some were designed to hold ten plates efficiently, others were designed to display a single plate.

It had gotten to the point that early on Vernon had started running out of space. Word spread slowly of his work and soon plate collectors from all over the world were contacting Vernon to see if he had any plate racks for sale. Eventually people tired of collecting plates and decided to just collect plate racks. Vernon's work was prized highly for his thorough design concepts and his wide array of style choices.

Vernon for his part was never particularly interested in the money or the collectors or even the art of plate rack making. He was just trying to make the perfect plate rack. Vernon wasn't sure if he was getting any closer, but it didn't much matter. He enjoyed building them and, all in all, everything was right and beautiful in the world.

Well, most everything was, at least. When the fallout hit Wayne, Yvonne and Rita had all been in a cell together and had been fused into a horrible three-headed mutant creature. It looked horrifying and the Rita and Yvonne heads both could roar frightfully. Fortunately, they seemed preoccupied with screaming and howling at the Wayne head, which just hang shame faced and occasionally let out a mournful wail.

It did however keep the neighborhood awake. Eventually the giant patrol robot would arrive and drive off the mutant into the darkness with its fire breath and death ray eyes. It always came back. The heads seemed to need to be seen. The Yvonne and Rita heads would bluster and roar louder when people were around, and the Wayne head would whimper all the more pathetically when it thought a sympathetic eye was nearby.

Behind them a teenage girl tagged along, letting out disgusted sighs and muttering the entire time. With each bestial growl or pitiful wail coming from the creature she would roll her eyes and complain through gritted teeth: "Jimmy's mutant parents don't embarrass him when the robots come," or "I never asked to be born to a three-headed mutant," or more simply, "You're ruining my life!"

After the reprimand from the girl the Yvonne head would hiss at the Wade head for embarrassing their daughter and ruining all their lives. The Rita head would join in the castigation and the Wayne head would begin to moan dolefully and the process would just restart until the robots arrived brandishing their eye lasers.

Vernon could hear the howling upstairs. It would probably go for another hour before the booming clamor of the giant robots would arrive to dispatch the creature for the night. RoboPurvis sauntered down the stairs, uninterested in the mammoth mutant outside and planted itself in the middle of floor to recharge a bit longer. Vernon carefully measured out a length of board and then compared the markings to his blueprint. Measure twice, cut once, Vernon thought to himself as he began his latest project.

At the end of the bench, covered in an oily rag with years of sawdust and dirt was an old rusty shotgun, both barrels still loaded, untouched and nearly forgotten. Next to it was a crumpled and faded piece of paper with little lines and checkmarks through long-illegible items of a list. Only two weren't checked off. The only one legible was scratched out, rewritten and underlined. It simply said "build plate rack."

Also by the author:

All the Stupid Little Children

All the Lights That Have Shone